I0770400

BELLS

THE BOYS OF CHAPEL CREST

A PREQUEL
BOOK 1.5

K.G REUSS

Formatting: Books From Beyond

Editing/Proofreading: The "Write" Editor

Cover Design: Moonstruck Cover Design & Photography, moonstruckcoverdesign.com

FOREWORD

Dearest Reader

You are about to embark on the story *before* Sirena. This tale is dark in nature. Please know your limits. At Chapel Crest, there are none. Anything and everything goes. Visit www.kgreuss.com for more information.

There are loads of twists and turns, so make sure you're taking notes if you're trying to decipher what will happen next in the series. We do have a Discord where you can join and freely discuss spoilers and theories with other readers. Simply join K.G. Reuss's Renegade Readers on Facebook and follow the instructions on how to get access to the Discord channel.

Welcome to THE BEFORE.

Happy Screaming.

-K

SIN

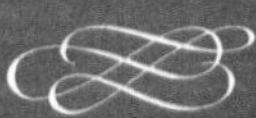

"*I* don't like her," Stitches said, glancing over to the blonde at the table next to us. She was staring down at a book and completely ignoring us.

"Not really your call," I muttered to him as she popped a pretzel into her mouth. "She likes me. I'm trying to get my shit sorted. She listens."

Church scoffed next to me. "She sucks your dick. That's about the only communication you two have with one another."

I gave him the finger, which made Ashes snort from beside Church who simply gave me a look that said he didn't give a fuck one way or the other what I did or why I did it.

We were students here at Chapel Crest. Or patients. I supposed it depended on how you looked at it. Chapel Crest was a fucking asylum academy, and I'd never let anyone tell me differently. We were all a million shades of fucked up here. There was a medical ward on campus where many of us went for therapy or an extended vacation if we lost our shit. It's where meds were handed out like candy and religion over science choked you.

If the pills wouldn't cure you, God would.

At least that's how it seemed to be here. Religion was a fundamental study for us all. It was the core of treatment and the core of recovery.

Good boys and girls who don't lose their shit and kill people got to go to heaven.

The rest of us got to go to Chapel Crest.

Our headmaster was a practicing doctor and a complete fucking cocksucker we hated. I knew the fuck was into experimental treatments and probably other shady business, but I'd never be able to prove it. None of us would unless we slipped and fell hard and ended up admitted into the medical side.

"I'm not saying it's my call, Sinclair. I'm saying I don't trust her. She's fucked up even more than we are," Stitches said, bringing me back to the moment as I stared at her from my seat. "I'm just trying to save your fucking heart, asshole. And your sanity."

"Ah, fuck sanity," Church said, getting to his feet and heaving his orange across the courtyard. It smashed into the side of Danny Linley's face. He immediately reached for his bleeding nose and stumbled away from where he was sitting.

Church looked back over at us and grinned, his blond hair falling into his eyes. "He was playing with his cock under the table over his pants. Fuck that guy. I'm trying to eat my hot dog here. He was ruining the fucking experience for me."

Stitches let out a huff of laughter. "Rumor has it he fucked some passed out chick at a party and got sent here instead of jail time because his old man is loaded."

"Aren't you into fucking the unconscious?" I asked, finally looking to Church who didn't look the least bit ashamed of who he was. Church was dark and twisted, much like the rest of us. He didn't display many emotions, at least not ones that brought warm and fuzzy to mind. If he could hurt it, smash it, break it, or kill it, that was what he'd do.

He leveled his green eyes on me. "The difference between Danny Linley and me is that the chick would fuck me awake and scream no to him."

Stitches jerked his thumb at Church. "He's got a point. If she'd fuck you awake, she'd fuck you sleeping. It's science."

I rolled my eyes at the two nut jobs as they high-fived.

I got to my feet, my sights set on the blonde.

"Be careful," Ashes said, his blue eyes roving over to the girl I was eyeing.

Isabella.

A complete fucking basket case, but she fucked and sucked and that's what I needed. I'd say she checked all my boxes. I liked her a hell of a lot, and I wasn't about to just overlook that since I never felt shit for girls before. Because of the way being with her made me feel, I kept at it, hoping maybe she was the cure for all the bad shit in my life.

"Fuck being careful," I said, turning to grin at my friends. The watchers. My ride or die posse. We ruled this place with an iron fist and giant cocks. No one fucked with us.

"Atta boy!" Stitches shouted. "Go get mentally fucked up. You need more of that."

I shook my head and gave him the finger as I walked away from our table. The moment I was at Isabella's table, a smile spilled onto my face.

"Hey, Bells," I said, grinning down at her.

"Sin," she answered in her silky voice, her dark eyes trailing over me. I liked her blonde hair spilling around her the way it was. Made it fun to twist my fingers in.

I nodded my head slightly. A playful smile spread over her pretty face as she got to her feet and followed me.

Lead me not into temptation but deliver me from evil.

A-fucking-men for crazy pussy.

BELLS

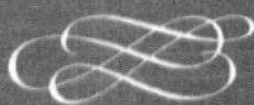

Sin pinned me to the wall, his gray eyes filled with lust. We'd found an empty room in the Bible studies area moments before. I smiled coyly up at him, knowing exactly how boys like him worked. He wanted it all and thought he could have it with me.

He was sexy enough that I was interested in trying. It helped pass the time in this fucking prison. He was good to me. Maybe not as good as I deserved, but he was a watcher and one of the best this place had to offer.

Plus, I needed him to get to what I really wanted.

He lifted me, and I wrapped my legs around his waist before he slid his latex-sheathed cock deep inside me, earning a soft groan from my lips.

"Why'd you wear the condom?" I breathed out as he filled me. "I'm on the pill."

"We're all on a lot of pills, Bells," he answered gruffly, thrusting into me.

I moaned softly, taking all of him. Sin knew how to fuck, and I relished in every moment he gave me.

"I hate the way it feels," I said between kisses. His tongue clicked against my teeth in our fervor.

I knew we were playing it safe. Neither of us needed to have a kid, but feeling his warmth deep inside me would have made these moments even better.

"Me too," he grunted, giving my asscheek a squeeze.

He didn't say anything else as he continued to plunder my pussy, dragging an orgasm from my body as I clenched around his long, thick, pierced cock.

Pierced cock.

I loved that about him. Tatted and pierced. Violent. And angry. I loved that he was angry.

I was angry too.

"Harder," I rasped, tangling my fingers in his blond hair. It had fallen out of the man bun he kept it in and cascaded around his shoulders.

He obliged my demand and fucked me so hard it hurt.

I winced before crashing my lips against his, earning a hiss from him when I bit his bottom lip. His fingers dug deeper into my asscheeks, making me whimper as he forced another earth-shattering release from me.

I cried out his name as I came hard on his cock.

His feral groan echoed around us as his release jetted out of him, leaving us both breathless.

He pulled out of me and placed me on my feet. I quickly adjusted my panties and let my skirt down as he tugged his condom off and tossed it into a trash can nearby before tucking his cock back into his pants.

"Mm, Sin," I cooed, dragging him back to me. "You're so fucking good."

He smirked down at me. "You're not too bad yourself. I like when you come on my cock."

I laughed softly and licked my lips. "Can I come on your cock later tonight?"

"Absolutely."

I swallowed and said what I was thinking, knowing it wasn't going to end well.

"I don't mind if your friends want to watch us. I know they fuck girls together—"

"You're my girl, Bells," he said firmly, his gray eyes flashing with the violence he kept so carefully caged. "You're not just one of the many who parade through our bedrooms. That means something to me."

I jutted out my bottom lip. "Promise you aren't fucking any of those girls? Melanie?"

"I'm not fucking any of them," he said, eyeing me. "And I don't plan on it."

"Do you watch?" I studied him for a response.

He sighed. "I haven't in a long time. I have you. I don't need to watch or participate."

I was treading into dangerous territory.

"Don't you ever just want to share me though? Maybe with Church?"

His eyes darkened, and he backed away from me. I reached for him, but he slapped my hands off him.

"No, I don't fucking want to share you with Church," he snapped at me. "What the fuck, Isabella? What is your obsession with my friends? Am I not good enough or something?"

"Of course you're good," I said, reaching for him again. He scowled but didn't push me away this time.

"What about you?" he grunted, glaring down at me. "Are you fucking any of the guys following you around like lost puppies here?"

I bit my bottom lip and stared up at him. "No."

He studied me for a moment, his features not as hard as they'd been moments before. "Promise, Bells?"

I frowned. I hated when he got needy and weak. His personality disorder left him all over the damn place. Most of those places I enjoyed just because they brought me joy. This one I didn't. At least not today. I wasn't in the mood for games.

"Sure. Yes. Promise," I said, pulling away from him. "You have the best cock I've seen on campus, so why would I want anything else?"

"You're just. . . I don't know. You act like you want Church," he mumbled.

Dante Church was gorgeous. All the watchers were. Tons of girls in this hellhole fantasized about them. Especially Church.

He only ever looked through me, not at me. I hated that. It pissed me off. He ignored me most of the time unless he was telling me to get the fuck out of the house they shared on campus. When I'd started seeing Sin, it was in the hopes I'd get closer to Church. It hadn't happened, and I'd made do with Sinclair Priest. He was delicious and toxic. His brand of insanity was fun for me. I liked stirring his pot and making him crazier.

I was certain he enjoyed doing the same to me.

"I care about you," Sin murmured. "You know that, right?"

"Can people like us feel those emotions?" I asked, peering up at him from beneath my long lashes.

"I feel them," he confirmed softly. "When I'm with you."

"Ugh." I pushed him away.

"Bells, for fuck's sake." He sighed. "Why are you like this?"

I pulled out my compact and applied more lip gloss to my lips. "Like what?"

"Just when I think we're getting close, you push me away."

I smacked my lips together and put my stuff into my purse and turned back to him.

"I care about you too," I said, liking and loathing the moment.

It was the fear in his eyes that got me. The want. The desire. But the fear that he'd lose me since he'd already lost so much in his life, from his father committing suicide in front of him and trying to take him with him to his mother tossing his ass into this asylum academy. That fear he seemed to have that no one wanted him made me desperate for his attention, even if he wasn't what I truly wanted.

But the weakness that came with it turned me off. The pleading. The hurt look on his face. I hated all that. But god, I fucking loved to watch him crumble. I suppose that said a lot about who I was, but it didn't matter. I liked to do what made me feel good.

He reached for me again and drew me into his arms. "I'm not him."

I stiffened in his hold before shoving him away. "Don't fucking talk to me about him!"

He remained wordless as I glared at him. He always liked to point out my daddy issues. It led to a fight every single damn time. I'd been with Sin since the start of the new academic year here. Several months of this was enough to drive me over the edge.

"Don't ever fucking talk like that to me again."

"OK. I won't." He held his hands up in surrender.

I was over this shit.

"Thanks for making me come," I muttered, pushing past him.

"Bells, come on—"

I didn't hear the rest of what he said because the door slammed shut behind me, and I left him there, my body trembling.

The last thing I wanted to talk about was *him*.

My father.

The man who sold my virginity for a line of coke. Who demanded he got to watch as part of the payment.

The one who hurt me so badly that it landed me in this fucking hell.

I'd regretted telling Sin about him moments before I'd finished the story of my life. It was one of the few times I'd ever opened up. Of course, I'd left out who my guardian was since it would ruin a lot of things I was trying to obtain. I'd been sworn to secrecy long ago on it, and there was no way I'd betray his trust. My guardian. The man who knew how to touch me and make me feel something real.

I made it a point to never speak of my past again though. Not to Sin, at least.

Maybe not to anyone.

Ashes danced around the burning barrel, his blue eyes wild through the flames as he tossed more stuff inside.

"He's happy," Stitches said, taking a hit off his joint. He blew out the smoke and passed it to me.

I took it and inhaled a drag, relishing in the high as it blanketed me.

"He's always fucking happy when he's setting shit on fire," I muttered, handing the joint off to Church.

"It's kind of beautiful," Church said softly. "I suppose we all have our *things*, don't we? Shit that keeps our insanity at bay." He took a hit off the joint. "I like gutting cute little forest creatures. Stitches likes beating the fuck out of people."

"And walls," Stitches added, taking the joint from Church and finishing it off. "Don't forget those."

"And walls." Church nodded. "Ashes has fire. And counting. He definitely counts a lot. Can't figure out why he's so shit at math though."

Stitches snickered as Ashes let out a loud whoop of joy and threw a tire into the flames. We came here off campus to his special spot in the middle of nowhere Michigan every weekend so Ashes could set shit on fire. It really did keep him sane. He was a pyro. He had control issues with it. He was like an addict. If he didn't get a fix, he'd completely lose his shit and probably burn the house down. . . with us in it. He tended to go off the deep end when it came to fire.

"And Sin." Church raised a brow at me. "Is self-loathing a thing?"

"It's my fucking thing," I grumbled.

Church flashed his wicked grin at me. I shook my head and let out a laugh.

"I fucking suck, man. What can I say?" I shrugged.

"To be fair, you do spend a lot of time being a pain in the ass. Always pissed off. You're a fucking grouch." Stitches gave me a playful shove. "When are you going to lighten the fuck up?"

"He seems a hell of a lot lighter than he usually is," Church said. "It's Isabella's pussy, isn't it? What is it like burying yourself inside a self-absorbed narcissist with daddy issues?"

"I don't know. I haven't fucked you yet," I shot back.

"Nice." Church gave me a sour look. "Prick. For the record, I'd be bending you over, Sinclair, not the other way around."

"Fight you for it," I said, rolling my eyes at him.

"We doing a dick measuring contest because we all know mine is the biggest." Stitches chortled, grabbing his junk through his jeans.

"All lies," Ashes called out as he approached, his face damp with sweat and smudged with soot. "I have the biggest cock *and* the best."

I snorted at him as Church and Stitches laughed loudly.

"What?" Ashes blinked innocently at us.

To be fair, we all had big cocks, but Ashes had a little something the rest of us didn't. His sanity. Or at least some of it. He was the only one of us, despite his illnesses, who could keep his shit together most days. I wasn't sure how he managed, but he did. I'd never tell him how strong I thought he was though, especially after everything he'd been through in his life. The last thing I needed was him bringing the compliment out though and smacking me in the face with it whenever we were having this conversation. A conversation which we tended to have a lot.

Maybe it was a guy thing.

Or maybe it was an *us* thing.

Didn't matter. We were family and loved each other. Nothing past that mattered.

"You guys know it's true," Ashes continued, looking back to his fire, a smile on his face.

I glanced at Church who was watching him, a smirk on his lips.

"Yeah. You're right. Your dick is the biggest," Stitches said, winking at me.

We liked to keep Ashes in good spirits, especially when he was riding his high from his flames.

I threw my arm around Ashes's shoulders and watched the fire with him in silence. Many minutes later, I finally spoke.

"Are you OK?" I murmured as Church and Stitches smoked more weed behind us and talked shit to one another. They were brothers. Adopted brothers. Church's old man adopted Stitches when we were kids to keep Church from going completely insane. I was pretty sure Everett, Church's father, knew exactly what Stitches was to Church. They were both the devil on one another's shoulders. Sometimes I wondered which one was worse, but at the end of the day, I knew Church held that trophy. He lacked warmth and compassion when it came to those outside our circle.

"Yeah, man. Are you?" Ashes didn't look away from his flames as they licked the night sky.

"Trying to be."

"Aren't we all," he muttered. "And Isabella? How is that going? For real. No bullshit."

"I like her. A lot," I admitted, looking at him. "She makes me feel... different. But she also pisses me off. Is that love?" I let my arm fall away from his shoulders.

He turned to me and cocked his head, his eyes sparkling in the dancing light of the flames. "I've never been in love before, but that can't be hate, right? Especially if it makes you feel something... good."

"Right. Can't be," I said softly, looking back to the fire.

I swallowed hard.

I couldn't deny I felt something for Isabella. It excited and terrified me. It made me feel almost human. My feelings were always hard to sort through, but I felt like maybe I was getting it right with her. That maybe this was how it was supposed to feel.

When I was a kid, my parents went through a nasty divorce after years of my old man abusing my ma. He'd always been good to me until the day he took me from her and tried to kill me before turning the gun on himself. I watched from the floor in a puddle of my own blood, a bullet wound to my chest, as he blew his brains out after calling my mom so she could listen as we exited the world together.

I had trust issues. I had personality issues. I hated getting close to anyone. All the doctors said I struggled with PTSD. That I'd developed mental issues from what I'd been through. Behavior problems. Anger issues. Everything that could go wrong with a kid happened to me.

My mom sent me off here, to Chapel Crest, after I scared her and her new husband too much.

All I had were my best friends. The watchers.

I looked around at my family, taking in their faces.

Each looked troubled in their own way, but it was our norm.

We needed more. I knew we did.

I hated to admit that maybe love was what we were missing. Each of us deserved it. At least those were words my therapist told me to tell myself on repeat.

I deserved to be loved.

I deserved to love in return.

I looked back to the flames.

I could definitely love Isabella.

A smile touched my lips at the prospect of having a special someone in my life I could bond with who wasn't one of the guys. Who I could tell all my thoughts and fears to. Who would understand me. Make love to me. Tell me I was worth it.

Isabella. . .

My Bells. . .

I couldn't wait to see her again.

BELLS

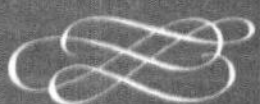

$\mathcal{I}$ watched as Church sat down at the watchers' table during lunch. He looked beautiful with his windswept blond hair, his Chapel Crest blazer open, and his collar unbuttoned. His icy green eyes took in his surroundings like a predator.

But he never looked at me.

I ground my teeth, wishing he would. Melanie was too close to him at his table. While I knew he wasn't with Melanie, the queen bee bitch who ran a lot of Chapel Crest when Church wasn't putting people to their knees, I knew he was fucking her whenever he got the chance. She was an easy lay, and rumor had it she laid with all of them. She'd even been with Sin before me.

I hated her.

I stared at Church as he raked his fingers through his hair.

Please, look at me. . .

"Hey," Sin's voice cut through my thoughts.

I smiled up at him. "Hey."

"I like your hair in that ponytail. It's good for tugging."

I blew out a breath and fixed the smile on my face as I noticed Church now talking to Melanie. My nails dug into my palms as I fisted my hands, my jaw tense. She raked her fingers through his hair.

"You OK?"

"Yeah. Why?"

Sin looked to where Church was sitting with Melanie and frowned.

"You seem. . . distracted."

I rolled my eyes at him. "Seems to me that maybe you're distracted. Do you want to argue with me or something?"

"No. I came to see you. Why are you upset?"

"Why do you always think I'm upset? You're being ridiculous," I snapped at him. My anger bubbled to the surface. I was chomping at the bit to drive my fist into the center of Melanie's face as she giggled at something Church said.

"I don't mean to be a dick, Bells, but did you take your meds today—"

I ground my teeth. "Of course I took my meds. I take them every fucking day, Sin."

"Easy. I'm just asking. You're really acting like a bit of a bitch."

"Oh, so now I'm a bitch?" I got to my feet as he stared up at me.

"Bells, that's not what I meant. There's a big fucking difference between acting like a bitch and actually being one. Come on." He reached for my hand. "Sit down."

I jerked my hand away from him. "I don't want to sit down. You're always ruining everything."

He got to his feet and stared me down. He towered over me by a good six or seven inches. I wasn't exactly short, but I wasn't as tall as he was. I never cared to remember his height, but I knew Church was well over six feet tall and Sin rivaled him.

Church.

I looked over at him again to see Stitches and Ashes had joined him. Melanie was at least paying attention to Ashes now instead of Church, which offered me some relief.

Sin's fingers found my jaw, and he forced my attention back to him.

"Look at me, not my friends," he growled.

"Your friends are more exciting than you," I said softly.

His fingers shook beneath my chin. Maybe I was being a bitch. Or maybe I really was just a bitch, but something about seeing him struggle to maintain his composure did something to me. Something I liked. That excited me.

I liked Sin. Mostly. It's just Church. . .

I sighed.

"I care about you," he said, his voice low. "Why are you being this way?"

"You care about me?" I raised my eyebrows at him.

"Yes, Bells. You know I fucking care about you. You're my girl."

"But you just *care*?" I narrowed my eyes at him. "That's cute, Sin." I made to step around him, but he snagged my hand.

"What do you want me to do?" He looked so vulnerable. I liked that. But I hated it. I wanted him to fight me. Church would fight me. I knew he would.

"I want you to man up and prove to me how much you *care* about me," I snapped at him. I didn't wait for his rebuttal. I ripped my hand free of his hold and stomped off but not before I cast a final look at Church.

My heart caught in my throat as his green eyes focused on me before he tore his focus away and looked to Melanie.

It wasn't a lot, but it was something.

He'd looked at me.

✝

TWO DAYS LATER, I trudged across Chapel Crest's campus, my excitement at an all-time high. Sin and I were getting along again, but that tended to happen whenever I stepped it up a notch. He'd crawl back to me on his knees and do something he thought was sweet for me. In this latest case, he'd brought me a bouquet of daisies with a sweet little note written inside a card with a photo of us he'd taken on his phone.

You're the bright spot in my life, Bells. I hope these flowers make you smile.

Always

Sin

They had made me smile. I hadn't even thrown them away. They were in a vase on my desk in my room next to the photo of us he'd included. It made me like him a little more, but it only made the feelings I had worse, as confusing as that was.

I wanted Sin. I knew I did. I knew I'd fight anyone who tried to take him from me. Being territorial was just who I was, even if my feelings weren't always strong about someone.

On the flip side of that, I knew I wanted Church too.

Badly.

The way I wanted Church couldn't even rival the feelings I had for Sin. Sin was my way to pass the time. Church was the way to pass eternity.

Church was meant to be mine. He'd been promised to me. . .

It angered me that Sin kept turning me down on inviting Church to join us. It was OK for him to do it with Melanie and Church, but it wasn't OK for Church to be with us. It didn't make sense.

I'd seen Church look at me. He'd *seen* me. I knew I was on his radar now.

I just needed to get Sin onboard. If Church wanted me, I'd be brought in. I wasn't all that into Stitches or Ashes, but I'd fuck with them if they all wanted me. I could be their girl. A queen in this fucking nuthouse.

I deserved to be a queen.

"Hey, Ding Dong," a deep voice called out to me.

I slowed to a stop and looked to the alley where the voice had called to me from.

Seth Cain stepped out from the shadows, his blue eyes dark, his full lips tilted into a smirk. His collar and first two buttons on his white uniform top were unbuttoned, half of it was untucked. and he wasn't wearing his blue Chapel Crest blazer.

"Fuck off," I snapped at him, hating his shitty nickname for me.

He'd been calling me that since I'd known him, and that had been a long ass time. I assumed it had to do with the sound a bell made.

"Aw, what's wrong with my favorite little narcissistic stalker today? Is she mad because a certain watcher isn't *watching* her back?" He stepped closer to me and cocked his head.

I glared up at him. He was tall like the watchers were. Built like them as well. I'd seen him working out in the gym a lot. And he ran. Often.

If he wasn't the absolute most insane person in here, I'd have been more interested in him. He went by the name Asylum. Rumor had it he'd carved out his stepfather's eyeballs with a fork and made him eat them.

There was sexy crazy then there was Asylum. He was beyond the scary crazy kind.

I was sure his crimes were worse than that of his stepfather, but I made it a point to stay away from him. My own problems were enough to deal with. Adding some psycho's shit to my list didn't fit into my agenda.

"Go fuck yourself, *Asylum*," I snarled at him.

He stopped in front of me and let out a soft laugh. "Fuck myself? *Ourself*, don't you mean, Ding Dong?"

Right. He also heard voices. He was a complete head case.

"Don't call me that."

He cocked his head in the other direction, his blue eyes so intense they bordered on creepy. I could practically see his crazy swimming around in the blue pools.

"I'm obsessed too," he murmured, ignoring my request. "I killed her. The obsession started after."

I swallowed thickly and looked around. We were alone out here. Of all the fucking times for the wards to be gone, it had to be now.

"You killed a girl?" I asked, wondering how far I'd get if I just ran. Judging by the open space and how in shape I knew he was, not far. I'd have to endure until someone arrived or he got bored.

He nodded. "She was the most beautiful girl I've ever known. Her hair was black as pitch and her eyes. . . so many colors. I see them still when I close my eyes. How big they got when she realized I was going to hurt her. She trusted me. She loved Seth so very much, and I . . . I loved her. Too bad she never got to know just how much."

"That's. . . unfortunate," I muttered.

A tiny, sad smile graced his pretty face. "One might say Sinclair is a lot like my girl was. Too trusting. Didn't see the forest for the trees. She was so focused on our safety that she neglected her own. Funny how those things happen, isn't it?"

"What aren't you saying?" I narrowed my eyes at him.

He began to circle me like a predator. I adjusted my backpack on my shoulder and kept my head high. Asylum was the sort of creature who preyed on fear. I'd not give him mine outwardly if I could help it. I'd dealt with wicked men before. I could handle him.

"She wants to know what we aren't saying," he said with a soft laugh.

Great, his voices were here too.

"We are saying that Sin is so focused on his love of you that he fails to see that you want one of his best friends. Ah, such a tangled web we weave when we first practice to deceive."

"Are you quoting Sir Walter Scott?"

"We are," he said, stopping in front of me. "But it's the truth, is it not?"

"I don't know what you and your invisible friends are talking about." I sneered at him.

He looked to his left and frowned. His lips moved, but I couldn't hear what he was saying.

He finally looked back to me. "That was rude, Ding Dong. *Very* rude. You should be more kind to those who are trying to help you."

I snorted at him. "Whatever. I need to go." I turned to walk away from him, but he called out to me.

"*If you play with fire, you're bound to get burned.* The watchers don't take prisoners. They take lives. Do not play games with them."

I turned back to him. "What?"

He cocked his head at me again, his blue eyes raking over me slowly. "Mm, yes. It's so sad."

"What is?" I demanded.

"You see, Ding Dong, I'm caught in a moral dilemma. I could continue to warn you off the watchers or. . . " He frowned.

"Or what?"

His blue eyes locked on me.

"What? Are you getting a message from the other side?" I rolled my eyes at him. He really was a fucking nut.

"Or I could let you meet your fate at the lake and get back what I lost," his voice trailed off, his brows crinkled tightly. He winced and smacked at his head. "Fuck. What the fuck?"

I stared at him, fascinated by whatever he was doing.

"*Rinny*," he called out softly. "Fuck. I-I didn't mean it. I wanted to protect you from the wicked. . ." He smacked his head again and let out a shuddering breath. "No. I wouldn't change it! Fucking stop! She can't come back. She fucking can't. She's dead. Dead. DEAD! In a box. In a box." He fisted his hair and tugged at it. "Stop!"

I backed away. If ever was a time to leave, it was now, but something about seeing this massive, beautiful guy cracking and breaking did something to me. He fascinated me.

He went to his knees, his fingers still twisted in his dark hair, humming some song I didn't recognize.

"Don't do it," he called out softly. "Ding Dong, the witch is dead. The witch is dead. The witch is dead. Or do it. . . and bring me back my dead. Dust in the wind. Ashes. Ashes. Ashes. Fire. You'll burn, Ding Dong."

That was enough for me. I hightailed it out of there. His type of crazy was too much for me today.

I'd leave Seth Cain to battle his demons on his own. It was a known fact Seth liked to get inside other people's heads and mess with them.

There was only room for me inside my head.

Hell if I'd let Seth Cain in too.

SIN

I thrust in and out of her body roughly, enjoying the warm, wet heat of her pussy as it clenched around my cock for the second time that night.

"Sin," Isabella moaned softly as I fucked her harder. She liked it rough, and I didn't mind giving it to her.

"Mm," I grunted, slamming into her pussy hard and jostling her tits.

"Fuck. Yes. More," she cried out.

There was no way in hell the guys couldn't hear me fucking her. I didn't have her over when they were home just because she was always watching Church. He didn't seem to have any interest in her, but the last thing I wanted to do was spend the night with my girl staring at my best friend. I knew he was a fucking stud, but come on. Cut me some slack.

Tonight had been different though.

She was all over me and acting normal. Like the girl I'd first met and liked.

"Harder," she rasped. "Fuck me harder."

I gave her what she wanted. Her pussy spasmed for me once more.

I spilled my load into the condom I was wearing and collapsed over her, my chest heaving.

"Fuck, Bells," I murmured, brushing my lips against hers.

She stared up at me, a small smile on her face. "That felt amazing."

My heart swelled. I'd put my all into it. I thought since she'd wanted me to try harder, the flowers, note, and some time in my bed might do the trick. So far, it seemed to be working.

I'd learned in my therapy lessons that I could be worthy of love, even on the days I felt like I was worthless. The road was so fucking hard to travel though. I felt like I was constantly beating myself up over it. I wanted to make this relationship work. Bells was the first girl I ever felt like this about. The idea of me fucking it up somehow weighed heavily on me. As much as I kept trying, it was hard to keep the intrusive thoughts of being a fucking waste out of my head, especially on days when she was pissed at me.

I nuzzled against her neck.

"I love you," I whispered. I'd never said that to anyone before. She would be my first, but I felt it so deeply, I knew it had to be love. *I was in love with her.* It all seemed to fall into place in that moment. I spent almost every waking moment thinking about her nowadays. It *had* to be love.

She stiffened beneath me.

Fuck.

I shifted and stared down at her, still buried in her heat.

"Bells?"

Her face was expressionless as she stared up at me.

I swallowed hard, nausea churning my guts. I'd just told her I loved her, and she was silent. It had been hard for me to come to terms with since I didn't feel like I could ever love anyone or they could love me back, but here I was, staring at the girl I'd fallen head over heels for and she was silent.

I fucked up. Again.

"Say something," I whispered. "Fuck. Anything."

She licked her lips. "I, uh. . . need to use the bathroom."

I blinked down at her for a moment before I pulled myself free of her pussy and rolled onto my back and stared up at the ceiling. She got out of bed and went into my attached bathroom, in the house I shared with my friends on campus, and closed the door behind her.

I breathed in and out slowly as I tried to calm my racing heart. Stitches told me not to ever tell a girl I loved her. I thought he was just fucking with me. I'd never considered love before Isabella. Never thought I had it in me. I was a twisted piece of work with some PTSD and a personality disorder. With depression. With a host of a million fucking broken things. I was fucked in the head. When I'd felt this feeling for her, I'd been elated because it was nice to feel something for someone instead of all the coldness. It made me feel human. It made me attach to her.

I sat up, my mood shifting from worry to anger, and disposed of my condom before I pulled my pants back on and tugged a t-shirt over my head. I settled on the edge of my bed with my fucking heart in my throat, the anger simmering just below the surface.

None of the progress I'd made mattered. Not if I didn't matter. I was never going to be fucking good enough for her. She made sure I danced that line for her though. I was at my wit's end. I didn't know how to make her love me back, and that fucking hurt.

I hated to hurt. To be broken by someone I thought cared for me. It probably stemmed from my old man telling me he loved me and treating me like he did only for him to kidnap me and put a bullet in my chest.

I tugged at my hair and looked to my ceiling. I needed to smoke. My nerves were shot. I got up just as Isabella opened the door to the bathroom and stepped out naked.

My heart jumped at the sight of her, and I silently cursed myself for those feelings.

"Sin?"

"What?"

She came forward and stopped in front of me. "I-I care about you too. It's hard for me to say the words. It scares me to say them. I don't want you to think I don't have feelings though because I definitely do."

Confusion rushed over me. "You-you *care*?"

She nodded. "I more than care, but the words. . . it's just scary."

"More than care? So like love? Or maybe close to love?" I hated how pathetic I sounded.

"All of that," she murmured, going up on her tiptoes and brushing her lips against mine.

I kissed her back, my heart thrumming happily in my chest again. She hadn't said she loved me back, but she did say she cared. I knew it was hard for her. I'd accept this answer because maybe I was fucking desperate to keep these feelings alive within me.

"Come back to bed," I whispered against her lips.

"Mm, ok," she said back, making my heart leap even further.

I shoved my pants down, and brought her back to my bed and dragged her on top of me. Quickly, I grabbed a condom out of my bedside drawer and sheathed my cock. She slipped back onto my waiting dick and rode me slowly, her lips on mine, her breathing heavy.

"Fuck, Bells," I groaned as she moved back and forth on me.

"You like this?" she asked between kisses.

"I love it. You're going to make me come. I don't want to come, yet."

"I want you to. I want you to come. Please," she rasped against my lips, her pace picking up.

I breathed out as she sat up, giving me a full view of her tits as she rocked on my cock. Everything inside me told me I shouldn't blow off inside her yet, but I felt the tingle of my impending release tease my dick as she raked her nails down my chest.

"Bells, I need to come—"

"Take off the condom and come on my pussy."

I swallowed, trying to control my cock from doing what it was threatening to do. Her pussy gripped my dick hard as she came, moaning my name.

I couldn't handle it.

Quickly, I rolled her onto her back and slammed into her heat hard and fast. Her fingernails tore into my back as she tried to keep me against her body.

I pulled myself free of her and tugged off the condom. A few rough strokes from my hand had me coming every-fucking-where.

In moments, I had her pussy painted white.

Breathless, I stared down at the mess I'd made before offering her a grin.

"Sorry," I said.

"I like it." She let out a giggle.

I chuckled and got off the bed to get her something to clean up with. In my bathroom, I wet a washcloth after washing my hand and went back into the room to find her running her finger up and down her slit.

My heart jumped, and I quickly wiped my come off her as she watched me.

"You probably shouldn't do that," I said, noting how she lightly fingered herself.

"Why?" She bit her bottom lip. "Does it make you want to fuck me again, Sinclair?"

I let out a huff of laughter. "Well, that and the fact I don't need you to get knocked up."

She pulled her finger free of her heat and gave me a coy smile. "It'll be fine. I'm sure."

I fucking hoped so.

I leaned down and kissed her lightly. She was quick to devour my kiss and drag me back down beside her on the bed.

And I was the sucker who let her.

BELLS

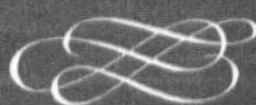

"Share, dick," Stitches shouted as Sin took a deep hit off his joint on the living room couch. I'd had sex with Sin again and we'd fallen asleep only to be woken by Stitches pounding on Sin's bedroom door and telling him they needed him for some video game.

I'd have been lying if I said I wasn't excited at the prospect of spending the evening with the watchers. Every girl wanted at least one of them.

I cast a quick look to see Church take a deep drink from a bottle of whiskey he had before he handed it off to Ashes who shook his head as he flipped his lighter open and closed on repeat. Honestly, I wasn't sure how anyone could put up with Ashes's incessant OCD or whatever the hell he had. He was certainly nice to look at, but he drove me a little nuts whenever he pulled out his lighter. And a little scared. I knew he was a pyro and struggled with it. I just worried his pyrotechnics also included people.

I mean, we were all here for a reason, and not any of them were good.

Sin handed off his joint to Stitches who smoked deeply before blowing out a cloud of smoke and letting out a shout.

Stitches was rough. Wild. Violent.

He reminded me a lot of Sin, except Stitches was part Hispanic and had tats pretty much all over his body. Even some on his pretty face.

"So, Bells," Stitches said as Sin tugged me against his body. "I heard you and Sin fucking."

"Man, stop," Sin grumbled as Stitches's dark eyes danced with merriment.

"You did?" I raised a brow at him, wondering if he was the only one who heard.

"Of course I fucking did. Pretty sure all of Chapel Crest heard you two. Is he really that good, or are you one hell of an actress?" Stitches shot a wink at Sin who flipped him off.

"Well, it wasn't all Sin. I have to give myself some of the credit," I said, licking my lips. I had a desire to know what Stitches's reaction would be.

Stitches snorted, unaffected by my attempt.

"Doubt it. Most chicks just lay there and expect to get off. Did you know a lot of chicks can't even get off with cock? Someone has to suck their clit to get them off."

"Stitches, man, stop," Sin said, an edge to his voice.

"Is that how it is for you?" I sat forward. "Your cock isn't good enough to get a girl off?"

Stitches narrowed his eyes at me. "Guess you'll never know, huh?"

I rolled my eyes at him. He was as unaffected by me as I was by him.

I chanced a look to Church to see him and Ashes watching the exchange. There was a wicked sparkle in Church's eyes that did something to my body.

Sin dragged me back against his body, the move protective and irritating.

My moods shifted so fast, I had a hard time controlling them at times. Opting to take a deep breath to control my reactions instead, I snuggled against him, not wanting to fight tonight.

Well, not much.

Within hours, I was high with Sin while the guys played video games together. At some point, Church stopped playing to take a break and went outside. I cast a look at Sin to see him completely absorbed in the game he was playing.

Figuring it was my chance, I got to my feet and quietly left the room to follow Church to the patio.

I found him leaning against it, smoking a joint, his attention on the lake.

"Nice night," I commented as I approached.

He didn't even bother to look at me. "Could be better."

"How so?" I sidled up beside him as he leaned against the railing, taking in the way he smelled. So. . . outdoorsy. Maybe like cedar and fresh air with a bit of spice.

I loved it.

He said nothing and shook his head before blowing out the smoke from the hit he'd taken.

"Is there anything I can do to help?" I ventured softly.

It took him a minute to look over at me, but his piercing green eyes made my breath catch as they locked on mine.

"You could make me a sandwich," he said after a moment, a tiny smirk on his lips.

I blinked at him, completely shocked by his answer. I really thought he'd ask me for something else.

"Is that all?"

"What else could I want?" He studied me, the look on his face making my insides tighten.

"Well, pretty much anything," I said around a soft laugh. "But I'll make you a sandwich if that's what you want."

"It's what I want." He stepped away from me, his eyes fixed on me for a moment, before he turned to leave me alone outside.

I let out a shaky breath before I smiled.

He wanted more. He was just playing with me. That was OK because I liked playing.

I stayed outside for a few more minutes before I went back into the house to see the guys had stopped playing and were just chatting in the living room. I went straight to the kitchen and looked for the bread, finally finding it in the cupboard.

I had no idea what sort of sandwich he wanted.

I should have asked outside. Damnit.

Clearing my throat, I called out to him. "Church?"

Conversation halted in the living room as I stood holding a piece of bread in the kitchen.

"What kind of sandwich do you want?" I finished.

"Cock meat. It's his favorite," Stitches chortled.

Ashes snorted.

"We have ham in there. Or turkey. Surprise me," Church said, throwing a pillow at Stitches who caught it while laughing.

"You're getting my girlfriend to make you food?" A sour expression crossed Sin's face.

"I'll make you one too," I said, hoping I sounded cheerful and not irritated.

A smile touched Sin's lips. "Ham and cheese."

I turned to get to work, but Stitches interrupted me.

"I'll have a peanut butter and jelly. Ashes will take the cock meat since Church wasn't hungry for it."

"Man, fuck you," Ashes said, swatting at Stitches who laughed loudly again.

I wanted to be annoyed, but I was grateful that Church was giving me this chance. And that Sin was letting it happen.

Baby steps.

I set to work making the sandwiches, making sure to take my time with Church's. I slopped Stitches's peanut butter and jelly together, not giving a damn that jelly was running out the sides in a sticky mess.

Quickly, I took their food back to the living room and gave each their plate and settled in beside Sin, who bit into his sandwich and chewed.

"What a fucking mess," Stitches grumbled. "How the fuck do you screw up peanut butter and jelly?"

I ignored him as I waited for Church to try his sandwich. He opened his mouth and bit into it and chewed, his expression not changing and his actions remaining just as tense and overpowering as they always were.

"Mine doesn't have any meat in it," Ashes said softly.

"Well, if it's peanut butter and jelly then that's a good thing," Stitches muttered. His nose wrinkled as a glob of grape jelly splattered onto his plate.

"I said turkey," Ashes mumbled. "I, uh, guess it's a lettuce sandwich. . ."

Church swallowed and put his sandwich back on his plate and pushed it to Ashes. "Here. Have mine."

I breathed out evenly, feeling a little deflated, but that was fine. It was all fine. It was just Church teasing me, trying to get me to play the game harder that he was playing with me. I could do it. Whatever he wanted.

"This is good. Thanks," Sin said, reaching out and giving my thigh a squeeze before he went back to his sandwich.

"It'll get better," I whispered, catching Church's eye.

He stared me down for a moment before turning his attention back to Stitches who was licking jelly from his fingers.

It would definitely get better. I'd make sure of it.

CHURCH

I stared out at the lake, my fingers sticky from the blood on my hands. I'd killed a squirrel in the woods on my run and hadn't bothered to wash its blood off yet. I probably wouldn't either. There was just something about having the dead's blood beneath my nails that made me feel. . . alive.

I blamed those fucked up thoughts on my life being what it was. I knew death all too well, and I knew the steps it took to get there.

Whether I wanted it or not, that's just how my life was. You didn't grow up as Everett Church's son and not know how to kill. How to not find joy in it somehow. I was born and raised to have drying blood beneath my fingernails. Nothing was going to change that.

I felt her before I saw her.

Every hair on my neck stood on end.

I imagined people had that reaction whenever I was around too.

Isabella didn't scare me though. I found her interesting. Not necessarily in a good way. More like in the way a bug on fire will hold your attention as you fry it beneath a magnifying glass on a hot summer's afternoon.

You knew she was fun to play with but lacked any sort of purpose past the fun.

"Sin isn't here," I said, not bothering to turn to look at her.

Her soft footsteps carried over the patio before she stopped beside me.

"Oh," was all she said as she stared out at the lake.

We were both quiet for a moment before I spoke.

"We both know you're not looking for him though. What do you need?"

She was quiet for another moment before she spoke. "I thought maybe we could hang out."

"I don't *hang out* with anyone aside from the watchers." I looked over at her to see her studying me. There was something in her eyes that made me feel strange. I wasn't sure what that something was though. It wasn't *like*. It was more like pity perhaps.

"You're not a watcher," I finished. "See yourself out. I'll tell Sin you stopped by." I pushed off the railing and turned to go, but her hand shot out and latched onto my forearm. I ground my teeth tightly and looked to her. "No one fucking touches me either."

"Sorry," she said. She didn't take her hand away from me though which I found even more interesting. "I just. . ."

"I know what you want," I said, taking a step closer to her.

She stared up at me with wide eyes and parted lips. As far as looks went, Isabella wasn't bad at all. In fact, she probably gave Melanie, the chick we currently fucked with, a run for her money.

I stopped as our bodies nearly touched.

"What do I want?" She peered at me, not looking the least bit scared.

I smirked down at her. "Don't play stupid with me, Isabel."

"Call me Bells."

"Bells," I murmured, reaching out and rubbing a strand of her hair between my thumb and forefinger. "Sin doesn't share. I don't particularly care to either."

"You share Melanie," she said, her voice thick and laced with want as she breathed out.

I chuckled softly. "We pass her around like a joint. That's all. Is that what you want? To be our whore?"

"I just want. . ." her voice trailed off.

"You don't know what you want. That's the problem." I let her hair fall back to her shoulder and stepped away from her. "Come find me when you do. Leave."

"Church—"

"Fucking *leave*," I snarled at her. "Don't make me tell you again."

She visibly swallowed before turning and darting off the patio. I watched as she disappeared down the path through the trees and let out a sigh.

She was fucking trouble.

I knew she was.

Truth of the matter was, I wasn't really attracted to her. Sure, she was nice to look at and had a decent set of tits, but she didn't captivate me at all. She piqued my interest but nothing that made me desperate or ravenous to have her. No girl had ever made me feel that way.

Plus, she was Sin's girl. We didn't share our girlfriends. It wasn't like we'd all had a bunch of them. Usually, it was just Melanie being passed around or some other unstable chick with daddy issues. Getting tied down wasn't something I was interested in. The fact Sin had decided to pursue this relationship had been a huge surprise given his issues with intimacy and getting close to people.

But whatever made him happy. Or less crazy.

As for me, there wasn't a girl out there I'd met yet that made me feel happy or less crazy. Or more crazy. Because really, if she didn't make me insane, she wasn't the one.

At the end of the day though, Bells had me curious. I'd fuck her with Sin if she wanted, but Sin had to be down with it. If he wasn't, then it wasn't going to happen. The last thing I wanted to do was fuck my best friend's girl and hurt him.

I just wasn't that kind of monster. Not really, anyway.

If he wanted me to kill her, that was a completely different story.

I smiled at that thought.

Maybe he'd want me to do that for him. Either idea I'd be onboard with.

I was fucked like that.

SIN

$\mathcal{I}$ shoved Danny Linley hard against the brick wall as his beady eyes darted around, sweat dotting his forehead.

"What the fuck are you doing?" I snarled, my forearm digging deep into his throat as he shook beneath me.

"N-nothing—"

"I saw you looking at her. *Isabella*. You were touching your fucking dick, you sick fuck." I pressed my arm harder into his neck until he wheezed, his face reddening.

I couldn't help myself. All I could think about was killing this weasel fuck after seeing him jerking his dick behind a bush while watching Bells eat her lunch beside me. I'd rushed the bush where he was and now here we were, his face red and his dick hanging.

"You're a sick, twisted piece of garbage." I growled at him. "You don't deserve the fucking air you breathe. Is this what you do? Jerk-off behind bushes and watch women?"

"I-I can't help-help it," he choked out. "My disorder—"

"Fuck your disorder." I slammed him against the bricks again, earning more tears and snotty sobs from him. "You do know what's right and wrong, don't you?"

He shook beneath my hold but didn't say anything.

"Of course he knows," a soft voice called out. "We all know right from wrong. But sometimes wrong feels *so* right. Right, Danny?"

I looked to my left to see Asylum standing in the shadows looking sinister in his Chapel Crest uniform, his black hair a wild mess. He stepped out of the shadows and approached slowly. This fucker was crazy. They said he was schizophrenic. Heard voices. Saw shit. Talked to the monsters only he could see.

Asylum, or Seth Cain, was a creepy fucker with his piercing blue eyes and twisted smile. Rumor had it that he popped out his stepdad's eyes and forced him to eat them after tying him up.

As watchers, we worked around Asylum. For as crazy as he was, he never had a shortage of bitches worshipping at his feet. He'd have been one of us if he wasn't so damn. . . odd. I knew he would have been.

Of course, none of us could stand him either, so that was another issue.

"Get lost, Asylum," I snapped. "This doesn't concern you."

He stopped beside me and cocked his head as he took in the scene.

"You know what's so funny about this situation?" he finally asked.

"Enlighten me." I narrowed my eyes at him.

A tiny smirk cut his lips up as he reached out and brushed a piece of Danny's hair away from his sweaty forehead.

"It's that you're punishing him for the wrong reason."

I ground my teeth. "He was jerking off over here while watching my girl."

"*Your* girl." Asylum chuckled. "Ah, if only."

I was tiring of Asylum's bullshit and it had only been a few minutes since he'd arrived. He needed to get lost so I could get the fuck out of there.

"Fuck off," I said, focusing back on Danny who was still shaking like a leaf.

"P-please," Danny stuttered.

"Please what?" I demanded. "What do you want, you fucking piece of shit?"

"Just tell him who you were really looking at. Quickly. I'd like to have his undivided attention once you're done." Asylum leaned against the wall next to Danny and winked at me. "I'm talking about you, man bun."

Fucking prick.

"I-I can't," Danny wept. "H-he'll kill me."

"*I'll* kill you," Asylum said easily. "If you don't. I'm growing bored. My mind tends to wander to darker places when that happens."

I slammed Danny once more against the wall. "Who the fuck were you jerking off to? Last chance before I feed you your own cock."

He sobbed for a moment before he finally sputtered out, "You."

I froze for a moment before I released him. He fell to a knee, his dick out and hard, much to my disgust. I thought it had gone limp when I'd attacked him.

"That wasn't so hard," Asylum proclaimed before his blue eyes darted to Danny's hard dick. He cocked his head. "Or maybe it was."

He let out a cackle as I balled my hands into fists. Asylum had a way of knowing things. We always figured it was just him getting lucky or knowing how to read people. God knew he spent enough time watching everyone.

"Get the fuck out of here. If I catch you doing that shit again. . ." I didn't even know what the hell to say. The guy disgusted me.

Danny was on his feet, trying to hitch his pants up as he ran off, without a look behind him. I rounded on Asylum.

"How did you know?"

He shrugged and pushed off the brick wall. "Danny is a sex fiend. And you're pretty. Made sense."

I sighed. "What do you want? I know you weren't lurking in a dark corner hoping to get a look at Linley's cock."

He chuckled. "You're right. Definitely not my type. I like pretty, dead girls with colorful eyes," he mused, stepping around me. "Anyway, I did want to talk to you. Your girlfriend."

"What about her?" I was already on edge.

"Do be careful. It's the pretty ones that can drive us insane."

"Really? That's what you wanted to talk about?" I scoffed. "Listen, you fucking crack pot, I don't need your shit, OK? Bells and I are good."

"Are you?" He cocked his head. "Pay attention, Sinclair. Her demons fight yours."

"Whatever. Just. . . fuck off." I turned to walk away but hadn't made it very far when he called out to me.

"You say you love her. You're prepared to do anything for her. But consider your hatred and the road that could lead you down."

"I'm used to rough roads," I muttered, leaving him in the shadows, not knowing or giving a shit how he knew my feelings or why he felt the need to make his thoughts known.

✝

BELLS'S HEAD bobbed up and down on my cock. I twisted my fingers in her hair and breathed out. It wasn't the best blow job in the world, but my dick was getting sucked, so that counted as fantastic. Bells didn't like to suck cock. She did it, but it always felt half-assed. Today was no exception. She loved to get her pussy eaten though and I'd promised I would if she sucked me off.

I let my head fall back against the couch cushion in the living room as she sucked me. I moved her head faster on my cock, hoping to drive her deeper. She liked to keep it shallow on me which contributed to the poor performance.

It was fine though. I wanted to come, so I breathed out and focused on the heat of her mouth on my dick. Within moments, I was unloading into her mouth.

She took it all and pulled off me before she spit it onto my abdomen.

"What the fuck?" I looked from the mess on my abs to her face. She gave me a smile and shrugged before getting to her feet and pushing her panties off beneath her uniform skirt.

Sighing and irritated, I got to my feet and went to the bathroom and cleaned up. She always did that shit. Never swallowed me even though I always swallowed her. Annoyed, I went back out to find her on the leather couch with her legs spread, her finger sweeping up her heat.

Immediately, my annoyance disappeared. She had a way of doing that. Driving me nuts only to bring me back to my knees for her.

And so there I was, on my knees, staring at her glistening pussy.

"Are you hungry?" she asked softly.

I licked my lips and nodded.

She let out a soft, sexy laugh. "Then eat me, Sinclair. It's my turn to come in your mouth."

"I can't. Let's go to my room. The guys could come in—"

She rubbed her clit. "So? Maybe I want them to see you eating me out."

I let out a huff of laughter. "Well, I don't want my friends seeing your pussy—"

"If your face is buried in it, they won't see," she said softly.

I smiled as I watched her rub herself. She did have a point.

"Please? It turns me on that we might get caught. I want to come so badly," she continued in a soft, pleading whisper.

Fuck it.

I pushed her hand away and buried my face in her wet heat and lapped at her. She moaned softly, spreading her legs wider for me.

She tugged my rubber band out of my hair and it cascaded around me before she twisted her fingers in it and gripped tightly, her hips jutting up to meet my mouth, a soft moan coming off her lips.

"Sin," she called out. "More. Faster."

I ate faster, my tongue flicking along her clit. I knew my tongue ring drove her nuts, so I varied my movements with it until she was smashing her pussy in my face and riding it hard and fast.

She came with a shout as I buried two fingers deep in her heat.

I lazily licked at her for a few more moments before her body went limp and she released me, her legs spread wide and her pussy bared for anyone who came in to see.

I grabbed her panties and shimmied them up her legs and put

them back in place. She gave me a pout when I pulled her skirt back down.

"What?" I asked, sitting next to her on the couch and bringing her into my arms.

"Why do you always try to keep me covered?"

"The guys might come in."

"So?" She looked up at me. "You guys screw Melanie together and other girls—"

I frowned at her. "They're not you, Bells. And I haven't fucked anyone in months. Not since we started seeing each other."

"I'm just saying it's not a big deal if they see. Church is supposed to be home by now. Would it matter if he saw?"

I crinkled my brows as I stared down at her. "Do you want Church to see me eating you out? Or for him to see your pussy?"

She shrugged. "I'm not opposed to it."

I blinked in confusion at her, trying to gather my thoughts.

"Bells, I'm not going to share you. I love you. You're my girl. Church has his own women. He's not getting mine."

She chewed her bottom lip for a moment. "Never?"

"No. Why the fuck would I let him see you?" I demanded, my anger blossoming.

"To spice it up! To have some fun," she said, her eyes flashing at me as she sat up. "You're always doing this. Starting fights with me."

"What?" I stared in disbelief at her. "I just ate you out and was holding you. You're the one—"

She rolled her eyes. "Typical Sinclair. Blaming *me* for something *you* did."

"What? I didn't fucking do anything—"

"I just want to have some fun."

"You're not going to fucking have it with my friend," I snapped back. "It's me and you, Bells. Not me, you, and him. Not ever. Why do you even want that? I thought you and I—"

"We are," she shouted. "It's always us. Maybe you're a little boring, OK? I like excitement. I've not been getting it with you lately."

I let out a snort. "Right, because you coming in my mouth moments ago clearly showed you weren't excited."

She scowled at me and got to her feet. "I just asked for a little fun. That's all. You took it too far and started this fight."

I got to my feet and stared down at her. "Bells, I don't want to fight. I love you—"

"I'm not dealing with your shit tonight. Either you want me to be happy or you don't." She turned on her heel, her hair whipping behind her. I didn't know what the hell I'd done wrong or how to even fix it.

"Bells," I called out. "Don't go—"

She didn't stop. She walked out the door and left me there to think about what I'd done wrong, my heart in my throat.

That was the problem though. I was clueless.

One thing I was sure of though. I wasn't going to fucking share.

BELLS

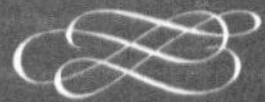

$\mathcal{I}$ was pissed.

All I'd wanted was for Sin to give a little. All he wanted to do was start fights with me and make me feel like I was the bad guy.

"You are the bad guy," Asylum called out through the darkness as I walked along the path. I hadn't seen him, but that was no surprise. He was like a shadow, always lurking behind people.

"Screw you, Seth," I said, picking up my pace.

He stepped out and walked beside me, shrouded in black. Goose-bumps rushed along my skin at his nearness. Seth was beautiful. Creepy and weird, but beautiful just the same.

"OK," he said. "We can do it right here if you want."

I stopped walking and faced him, the moonlight casting an eerie glow around him.

"What?"

"You want to fuck? I'll fuck you. I'm good at providing *excitement*." His eyes flashed in the moonlight.

Fucking Seth Cain? I knew Sin hated him. And right now, I was pissed at Sin for denying me what I wanted to try.

I licked my lips.

"Right here? Right now?" I asked, watching him.

He nodded wordlessly.

"In the middle of the path?"

He nodded again.

It wasn't exactly like Sin had been the only dick I'd ever been on. My entire life consisted of men's cocks, so what would make the difference tonight?

The only real difference was that I got to choose.

"What if we get caught?"

"Then we give them a show," he said softly.

I eyed him closely, wondering if he was even serious.

"Why? Why do you want to?" I took a step closer to him, definitely interested in anything that could piss off Sin right now, even if it meant I was fucking Seth Cain. Sin deserved to hurt just like I was.

"Let's just say I'm securing my future. Something tells me I need this," he said, his voice soft. Chills rushed over me again.

"What's the something that tells you? A little voice in your head?" I placed my hand over his chest, expecting to feel his heart hammering hard but was met with slow, even beating.

He stared down at me for all of a moment before he had me shoved against a tree, his hand over my mouth. My heart jumped into my throat as his eyes locked on mine.

"We don't talk about *them*," he hissed. "You do not know *us*, therefore you *do not speak* to us. Understand?"

I nodded wordlessly, my heart racing.

"I think we both need this," he continued in a growly rasp. "Your ending is my beginning, so let me fuck you, *Bells*, and put us both out of our misery."

"Are you going to tell Sin?" I asked as he withdrew his hand, his body still against mine. It hadn't slipped past me how hard he was.

He smirked. "Yes. Just not now."

"Perfect." I unbuttoned his pants. I was impulsive. Unhinged. Angry. I didn't know why I hated Sin so fucking much. I cared about him, but at the same time, I wanted to destroy him. It didn't make sense to me. He was decent enough. Handsome. He fucked like a god. He did anything I wanted... except let me have Church.

My anger flared red-hot as I wrapped my hand around the massive cock that belonged to Seth Cain.

"Fuck it," he said softly, indicating his length I held.

He hadn't moved or tried to fuck me. He was letting me do all the work. I stared up at him for a moment and decided maybe he was just into weird shit, so I turned around and bent over, my hand on his cock as I worked to guide his girth into me.

He still didn't help.

It didn't fucking matter.

I slid onto his cock after some work, sheathing him inside me with a soft moan.

Like a statue, he stood there as I rocked back and forth on him. I'd never fucked a guy who didn't participate past a hard cock before.

"It's no wonder he's having doubts right now," Seth mused softly. "Is this all you have, Isabella?"

Prick.

"Fuck you," I snapped.

He laughed softly. "I can see you're trying. I'm unimpressed."

"Well, if you'd help, you useless fucking asshole—"

My words were cut short as he gripped my hips tightly and slammed into me so hard I fell forward and smashed my face into the ground. I let out a cry of pain as he didn't even try to help me.

Instead, he crashed his hips against my ass as he fucked me hard and without mercy, driving my face deeper into the dirt.

I cried out, my nails digging into the ground as his cock continued its storm on my pussy until I was screaming his name and coming harder than I'd ever come in my life. His cock twitched deep inside me, releasing his load.

My breathing came in ragged gasps as he withdrew and dropped me unceremoniously onto the cold ground and tucked his dick away.

I said nothing as I laid there. That certainly hadn't been what I'd expected from him. Or myself.

I just fucked Seth Cain.

I cheated on Sin.

"And you don't feel an ounce of remorse," Seth whispered,

kneeling beside me. "Which makes it easier for me." He reached out and fisted my hair and brought my head off the ground. His eyes darted to my lips for all of a moment before he crushed his mouth to mine and kissed me deeply. His tongue rolled against my tongue before he bit me, drawing blood.

I tasted insanity in that moment. A true fucking nightmare.

He pulled away, stealing my breath, his lips lingering against the blood on my mouth.

"Open," he whispered against my lips.

I parted my lips for him, letting the madness drive me.

He spit into my mouth.

"*Now* fucking swallow."

I shook as he tightened his fingers in my hair, but I swallowed.

He smirked down at me. "You're a terrible fucking human."

My chest heaved as I stared up at him. "So are you."

He let out a soft chuckle. "I am. Now, it's time for the fun part. I hope you pray, Isabella."

"God left me a long time ago," I said thickly.

He released my hair and gave me a sinister smile. "I didn't say anything about God, silly girl."

And with that, he got to his feet and walked away before he disappeared into the darkness, leaving me with my panties around my ankles, a bleeding lip, and my pussy bruised.

But I was satisfied.

And that was all that fucking mattered.

SIN

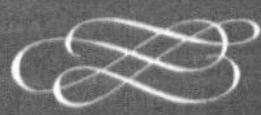

"You're giving her flowers?" Ashes looked from the flowers in my hand to my face, wincing.

"Yeah. I fucked up," I muttered. "It's my apology."

He sighed and shook his head. I'd told him about what had happened with Bells. Out of all my friends, Ashes was the one to go to when we needed a shoulder to cry on. Just as fucked up as we were, he still managed to keep his shit together. I hoped the day never came when he lost it. I was sure all his repressed rage at life would set the world on fire and render it to a kingdom of ash.

"Sin, you do understand you didn't do anything wrong, right? Isabella is. . ."

"She's what?" I demanded as we stood on the patio of our house overlooking the lake. "What is she, Ashes? Because as far as I'm concerned, she's what I deserve—"

"You deserve to be mentally and emotionally abused?" He frowned. "No, Sin. You don't. You don't see what she's doing to you. This relationship is toxic and abusive. You're not this guy—"

"This guy has never felt the way I feel right now. I-I love her," I finished softly. "That's all I know."

Ashes winced. "It's not the love you deserve. It's the love you're punishing yourself with."

I backed away from him with the flowers in my hand. "So be it."

I left him there, feeling sick to my stomach. Bells wasn't returning my texts. She wouldn't answer my calls or her door. She avoided me and was even missing therapy and classes. That wouldn't sit well once word got back to Sully. He was a prick and always looking for an excuse to punish students.

I walked to her dorm and pounded on the door.

Over and over.

"Bells. Come on," I called out. "Please."

I felt pathetic and disgusting begging like a pussy for her.

Just fucking answer me. . . please.

Don't. Don't fucking leave me. . .

Her door cracked open and my heart jumped into my throat as she peered out at me.

"Bells," I choked out. "Can-can we talk?"

She hesitated for a moment before she opened the door and stepped aside. I entered her room, and she closed the door behind me.

Her room was neat. Her bed was made with a lavender quilt. Her walls were bare, but I didn't expect anything to be there. Her family was trash and she had no friends that I knew of. It was just. . . us.

She needed me like I needed her.

"I'm sorry," I whispered, handing her the flowers. "I didn't mean to upset you. I-I just didn't want to share you. I-you're mine, Bells. I love you. I don't know what else I can say."

She took the flowers wordlessly and placed them next to her bed on the nightstand and looked at me.

I waited, my hands stuffed deep into my pockets, my eyes burning with the threat of tears.

Fuck.

"We're really different," she finally said. "I want different things."

"We're not," I said, stepping over to her. "I promise I want the same things—"

"I want excitement and fun. You want. . . greed."

"Greed? Bells, I-I just want you. I'm sorry if it seems—"

"Pathetic?" She raised a brow at me. "I want strength, Sin. You're only showing me weakness."

"You're my weakness," I whispered. "What do you want from me?"

She sighed and was quiet for so long I thought that maybe she wasn't going to answer and I'd fucked up further.

"I-I'm sorry too," she finally said.

I stared in shock at her. "What?"

"I may have overreacted. We're different, and maybe that's not such a bad thing."

"It's not," I said immediately. "It's what makes us who we are. It's a good thing."

She offered me a smile. "You're right."

"So. . . we're good?"

"I don't know. Maybe. We broke up."

"We. . . did?" I wasn't an expert on relationships, but I was pretty fucking sure we were just fighting and not broken up.

She nodded. "Yeah."

I moved to sit beside her. "I missed you. I. . .it doesn't matter to me if we broke up or whatever you want to call it. I want you now."

"Even if I slept with someone else?" She lifted her chin and locked her eyes on me.

My chest constricted at her words. "Did you. . ?"

"I was angry at you. I wanted it to hurt you. Does it hurt?"

I swallowed thickly. "Yeah, it fucking hurts, Bells."

"Does it change anything?" Her eyes skirted over my face.

I breathed out. "I. . . no."

"What if I told you who it was?"

"I don't fucking want to know," I whispered, wiping quickly at my eyes. "If you did, then you did. I still love you. I don't want you to go. I'm here. Nothing will change it. Not a name. Not shit. Regardless. . ." my voice trailed off as my chest ached with the knowledge of what she'd done and how fucking sad I was. Not just emotionally, but sad as an excuse for a fucking human.

But I didn't want to be alone. I wanted her. I loved her.

"Yeah?" She turned and ran her lips along my jaw. "You still love me?"

I let out a breath, desperate for her warmth. "Yes. I don't want to lose you."

"Mm, prove it to me."

"How?" I brushed my lips against hers, my heart banging hard. Fuck, I'd missed her. It had only been a few days, but I felt like my entire world had been crushed and the oxygen sucked out. I didn't know what the hell was the matter with me or why I was so damn clingy, but I was. I needed her. I fucking felt it in my soul. But I was also so afraid of her because now I was hurting even more at what she'd done.

I knew the power she wielded over my heart, as pathetic as that sounded. Over my damn mind. She could drive me crazy with just a smile, and she could shatter me with just a few words.

"Fuck me," she said, kissing me gently. "Show me how much you want me."

Gladly.

Within moments, we were both naked and breathing hard as we touched one another.

"I don't have anything," I whispered. "Do you?"

"You're proving it to me, remember?" she asked softly as she cradled my face.

I swallowed hard. "Bells. . . we need protection."

"Not if you love me and really want me. Not if you forgive me."

I knew what she was asking. I stared down at her, my cock so hard it hurt. I just wanted to be deep inside her where I could hide and bury my pain.

If I did this. . .

It could be forever. Something that would never leave me because she couldn't. We'd be bound forever.

I pushed deep into her wet heat, my cock bare and practically weeping joy.

"Fuck," I breathed out, feeling her warmth engulf me. Fucking girls bare wasn't something I ever did, but this was meant to be. I knew it was. "You're on something, right?"

I pulled out and pushed my way back inside her, relishing in the feeling.

"Yes. I am. It feels good," she said, clinging to me.

"Fuck yeah it does." I thrust in and out of her, relaxing a little. "So fucking good."

"I want you to come inside me," she said breathlessly, jutting her hips up to meet my deep thrusts. She let out a moan as her pussy began to tighten around me.

Fuck it. Fuck it all.

I sped up my pace, fucking her deep and hard, her headboard banging against the wall as she took all of my cock deep into her body, her tits bouncing for me, a smile on her face.

My name spilled from her lips as she came hard.

She wanted me. She loved me. It was just hard for her. God, I loved her too. So much. I loved having her.

I followed a moment later, groaning as I filled her pussy with my release, sealing our fate.

I pressed my forehead to hers, both of us gasping for air.

"I love you," I whispered as I balanced myself over her.

"I know," she answered.

I closed my eyes, praying someday she'd be able to say the words to me too.

"We're good now?"

"We're good," she said, cradling my face.

I relished in her touch, absorbing the warmth. When I rolled off her, I lay on my back at her side, staring up at the ceiling, turmoil sweeping through me.

I couldn't shake the feeling I'd done something really fucking bad despite my love for her.

She turned over and snuggled against me, her hand low on my abdomen.

I exhaled and pressed a kiss to the top of her head before I hugged her against me.

Despite all the fear now coursing through me at the implications of what we'd just done, I was here. I wasn't fucking leaving. She was my girl.

"Tell me you're mine, Bells."

"I'm yours, Sin," she said softly, hugging me against her. "Promise. Until the day I die."

I smiled at that.

"I'm yours too. Never anyone else's."

She chuckled softly. "Perfect."

And it was. Or would be.

It had to be. Anything less than that would fucking ruin my existence.

BELLS

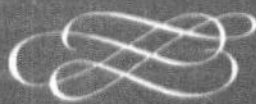

"How is paradise?" Asylum asked as he fell in step beside me. It had been a few weeks since I'd fucked him.

"Probably the same as hell," I answered. "It's a matter of perspective."

"I would agree with that," he said as we stopped walking down the wooded path through the forest.

I'd finished classes and therapy for the day and planned on getting some fresh air. I was meeting Sin later that night at his place. When we'd made up two weeks ago, he'd promised to have me over more and let me get to know his friends.

It was all I wanted really.

And to make him suffer like he was making me suffer.

I knew he didn't want me around Church, but he didn't understand how important Church was to me. To what we could all be together if he'd give it a chance.

But I knew what would happen.

I wanted to revere Dante Church and smash Sinclair Priest beneath my heel for making me feel so fucking trapped. Dante would never trap me. I knew he wouldn't. All the men in my life had trapped me. Tied me up. Hurt me. Beat me. Fucked me.

"You have a really shitty outlook," Seth said, breaking through my thoughts. "It would be a shame if Sin ever found out."

"He will," I said with a shrug. "Someday. All our skeletons tumble out of the closet eventually."

We continued to walk in silence for a moment before I asked the question that was burning on the tip of my tongue.

"How do you do that? Get inside my head and know what I'm thinking?"

We stopped and faced one another.

He cocked his head at me, his dark hair falling across his forehead.

"Why do you think I know what you're thinking?"

I rolled my eyes at him. "Because you do. Don't play stupid, Seth."

"Asylum," he corrected softly. "My name isn't Seth. It's Asylum."

"Whatever," I muttered. "How do you get inside my head like that, *Asylum?*"

"The wicked are always easy to figure out. It's not a parlor trick. You're just. . . simple and vengeful."

"You think you know," I muttered, hugging myself and frowning. Ugly memories attempted to invade my mind, but I shoved them away and locked the door.

"But I do," he said, blinking innocently at me. "The only man who was ever kind to you touched you when he shouldn't have. He made you believe it was real."

I swallowed thickly, tears springing to my eyes.

"It was real."

"It wasn't or he wouldn't have left. Besides, you were a child, Isabella. You didn't know. I've been there too. So has. . . Seth."

I scoffed at him and quickly wiped at my eyes. "You're nuts."

"Says the nut."

I shook my head and looked away from his piercing stare. "How did you know any of that? My records are sealed."

"They're sealed because Everett Church made them that way."

I winced at the use of the name of the man I loved.

"He doesn't love you."

"He does," I snapped at him. "He just. . . can't right now. He told me his son would love me in his place. That's my job. To love him. To make Everett happy. To get Church to join and then Everett will take me back. I'd have both him and Church—"

"He never saved you," he continued, ignoring me. "You know that, right? His touch. His kiss. *His cock*. None of it was to save you. It was because he's fucked in the head and you were a plaything to him."

"Shut up," I snarled at him, balling my hands into fists.

"I'm right and you know it. That's why you want Church so badly. You think you can have with him what you once had with his sick, twisted father. That you can reunite with a monster and create a monsterdom with the two biggest ones on the planet. Church doesn't even know his father owns you. It's a dirty secret you never told him. He has no clue you're his adopted sister who was kept in a cage to be taken out and played with whenever Everett let his demons out to feast. You were a fucking child, Isabella. A CHILD. It wasn't right!" His chest heaved as he stared down at me. "It's not fucking right."

I swallowed. "It was all I knew. It was the only time I was ever happy."

"You were seven."

"*And I was fifteen.* It doesn't fucking matter the age. I know what he meant to me. He saved me. He promised me—"

"He drowned your beauty and left his wicked behind. He turned you into this fucked up girl. You were payment for his sick games because your real father hated you too. Just like all the men your mother dragged home behind her. He gave you his sickness. I know. I know because he fucked with me too! Me too, Isabella!"

I glared up at him, noting the pain pinching at the corner of his eyes.

"Don't blame him for your wickedness, Asylum. We both know you were born, not created."

He let out a soft, sinister laugh. "I was born crazy. I was made insane. Get your facts right."

"So did you ride Daddy Everett's cock too?" I asked, stepping closer so my chest brushed against his.

He let out a soft huff of laughter. "I hurt the men who touch me. If he's still able to walk, then you know the answer to that."

I nodded. "Right. You pop out their eyeballs and feed it to them."

"Something like that," he said softly. "We do tend to do dastardly things when we're angry."

"We as in *us?* Me and you?"

A tiny smirk cut his lips upward. "No, *we* as in *us.*" He pointed to his head. "Right, Seth? We're fucking insane! We're nuts!" He let out a loud laugh, his body shaking with it. "We had to help the evil men until we became stronger. Until we overcame the wicked!"

I watched as he spun in a circle, his arms wide, his blue eyes bright. Laughter bubbled out of him as he spun.

I figured he had multiple personalities. I hadn't really thought much about it until that moment as I watched him spinning on the path, a crazy look in his eyes.

He finally stopped spinning and faced me again. He cocked his head and let out a bark of laughter, his eyes bright. Despite his crazy, he looked. . . happy.

"You know it's true. Something big is coming," he said softly, his words so fast I nearly couldn't catch them. "I promise it is. Just have faith."

"Who are you talking to?"

He snapped his gaze to me. "Seth."

I blinked at him. "Right. You, uh, have multiple personalities then? That rumor true?"

He smiled and looked to his left. I followed his gaze and saw nothing.

"Some rumors are true. Some are simply. . . misunderstood. Some are our deepest, darkest secrets."

"So who fucked me the other night?"

He snapped his attention back to me and smiled. "I did."

"And that would be Asylum?"

He nodded. "Seth would never fuck you. He's picky about his bitches. Besides, he's not really here right now. And honestly, I wouldn't have fucked you if I didn't know what I think I know."

I rolled my eyes at him. "And what's that?"

"That you're not here for a long time, just a good time." His smile faltered. "I'm sorry about that in a way. In another, I know it's taking *us* somewhere good. I'm trusting in that. It's just you won't be here for it."

"And where will I be?"

"Dead," he whispered. "And forgotten."

I swallowed thickly. "Fuck you."

"Already did."

"I hate you."

"I know." He cocked his head at me. "But you shouldn't. I'm just helping fate. It needs my help sometimes." He nodded to my stomach. "It's too bad. It really is. Everything happens for a reason, Isabella. Every frantic whisper. Every scream. Every death. All of it. This time, I get to benefit."

I was done with his brand of crazy. He made me feel like I needed to scream and tug my hair out.

"OK." He nodded. "This is goodbye then. Enjoy your night. Give Sin my love."

My phone buzzed in my pocket and I turned away from him to answer it, needing a moment to breathe.

"Hey, you want pizza?" Sin asked. "We were thinking of ordering in. Figured I'd ask."

"Yeah, that sounds great," I said, putting false cheer into my voice.

"Cool. I'll see you soon. Love you."

"Bye." I ended the call and turned to tell Asylum he could tell me what the hell he was talking about or just fuck off, but he was gone, the woods around me silent.

I sighed.

He was a weirdo.

I'd have regretted fucking him if it didn't make me feel good to know I'd done it.

He's just trying to scare me. It's what men do to good girls like me.

With that thought in mind, I shoved Asylum's words out of my head and continued down the path, the eerie feeling of being watched sticking with me until I reached Sin's house.

I turned to look back at the darkening forest and could have sworn I saw Asylum disappear into the shadows.

A shiver raced over me.

Fuck that nut job.

Well, not again, but seriously, he could piss right off. We'd had our fun. It was time for the next round. I knew he was just as twisted as I was. We were both tangled in the web Everett Church spun. The only difference was, Everett loved me and simply used Asylum's crazy to his advantage.

"I thought I saw you," Church said, answering the door.

My heart fluttered at the sight of him.

"Hey," I said, smiling up at him.

He raised a brow at me and stepped aside. "Sin is in the living room."

I brushed past him, dragging my fingers along his hand as I went.

I could have sworn he was smiling too.

BELLS

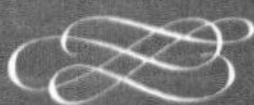

Weeks passed by, and I managed to hang on. Sin had relaxed quite a lot and wasn't nearly as clingy. I noticed with him that when he felt safe, he was easier to deal with. Of course, I did like getting him upset from time to time because it made me feel like I mattered since he'd always plead and apologize to me and beg me to love him.

I still hated and loved that about him.

We'd not had sex without protection since that day in my dorm.

It had been stupid on my part to let him inside me like that, but I liked to push his boundaries. And Sinclair Priest had a lot of them.

Of course, I'd also fucked Asylum.

His words still brought nightmares to my sleep.

Telling me I was going to die.

We all died at some point. I knew guys like Asylum. They liked to scare girls. Threaten us with things like death and pain. I was too used to that stuff, so it wouldn't work on me. At least that's what I kept telling myself.

He'd been wrong about Everett though. While I knew falling in love with him was a bad idea, I also found it to be good because he'd promised me Church, His son. He promised I'd get to keep him if I kept quiet and did what I was told. That I'd have both him and Church. The idea of having two of the underground's most powerful men did something to me. I wanted it. I wanted to rule and hurt people like they hurt me.

I could do that. I could hang onto Sin and play my games with him if it meant I'd get Everett and Church in the end.

The prize was worth it.

Dante Church reminded me of his father in so many ways. Handsome. Muscular. Strong. Powerful. Rich. He was feared.

I loved that. He even scared me.

"If you can break him down, he's yours. Bring him to me. For our kingdom, my sweet, beautiful princess."

Everett's words rushed through my mind as I thought back to the night just months ago when he'd fucked me in his office. It wasn't the first time he'd been in my ass, but it was the first time he'd stayed to hold me after. To make promises to me. To tell me secrets. Dante was fighting his responsibilities in Everett's organization. He was disappointing Everett. If I could get him to fall in line, I'd win.

I liked winning. I was banished from Everett until I returned with Church on our side.

"That was good," I murmured, kissing along Sin's chest as I lay next to him in his bed that night. He'd started letting me stay over more.

"Yeah it was," he answered, giving me a squeeze.

"I'm really thirsty," I continued, reaching down and stroking his cock. The thing about Sin was he was quick to bounce back. I appreciated that about him.

"You won't get anything from there," he said, laughing softly. "You've drained me, Bells."

I smiled. Sin was good with his cock. I'd give him that.

"Then I guess I'll just have to go get something from the kitchen," I said, going up and kissing his lips.

I made to break away from him, but he was quick to drag me back and deepen the kiss. I fell into it, finding it nice. The way Sin kissed was something truly amazing. He was just rough enough to hurt, but so fierce you knew you couldn't fight him and win.

All in all, he was pretty perfect at it.

The best kisser I'd ever encountered.

Not that I had a lot to compare it to. Most of my encounters didn't involve kissing.

"I'll get it," he said against my lips.

"Nonsense. You did all the hard work tonight. Let me." I nipped at his bottom lip, making him chuckle softly and release me.

Quickly, I got to my feet and tugged on my robe that I'd brought in my overnight bag and left the room and went to the kitchen.

I dug around in the fridge until I unearthed two bottles of water. When I turned, I came face to face with Church.

A gasp of surprise left my lips as I stared at him through the dim overhead sink light.

"Hey," I managed to say.

"Hey." His face remained expressionless as he stared at me.

"Um, I just came out to get some water."

"Clearly," he answered.

"Right." I licked my lips and placed the water on the counter and cleared my throat. I never got chances to be alone with him. I had to take every opportunity I could. "I'm staying over tonight."

"You stayed over last night too," he said, still standing in the same spot, his white t-shirt hugging his body, his dark pajama bottoms hanging low on his hips.

"You noticed."

"I notice when there's a girl staying in my house," he said.

I smiled. "I didn't know that."

He surveyed me but said nothing.

I offered him a smile. He was definitely like his father. Emotionless.

I liked that because when they broke, they broke hard.

Even Everett had whispered he loved me to me.

And if Everett Church could say such sweet words, I knew his son was capable of it. He just needed the right motivation.

"I like staying here," I said, stepping closer to him.

He said nothing, his green eyes trained on me.

"I like being close to you," I ventured softly. "Fucking Sin and knowing you're nearby and can hear me. Do you hear me?"

He continued to stare wordlessly at me.

I reached down and undid the belt on my robe and let it fall open, revealing my naked body to him.

"What are you doing?" he finally asked, his gaze sweeping over my naked body. Desire rushed through me, knowing he was taking in my breasts and pussy.

"Nothing. And everything." I leaned in, my breasts brushing against his t-shirt. I moved in closer when he didn't move away from me.

"You can touch me, Dante."

"Don't call me Dante," he said softly. "That's not a name I'll let you use."

"Church," I murmured, running my hand along his abs, my pulse pounding hard and my pussy dampening at the thought of him touching me back. "Sin is in his room."

"And?"

"And we're not."

He let out a soft laugh that held no humor.

"You're Sin's girl. I don't fuck with any of my friends' girls."

I was losing him. I wanted to scream. Instead, I steadied myself and moved my hand lower until I was at the top of his waistband.

"Sin and I are playing a little game. He has this fantasy that he walks in on you fucking me. He doesn't want to talk about it though. He wants it to be a complete surprise so he can feel everything when it happens."

"That a fact?" Church murmured.

"Mmhmm. Do you want to play with me. . . Church?"

He stared down at me, his eyes glinting.

"How do we play?"

"Well, we never talk about it. It's like a fun little secret all the things we do until we get caught. Then when Sin finds us together, he will join in. Would you fuck me with him?"

He was quiet for so long I was scared he wasn't going to answer me.

"I'm. . . intrigued."

My heart leaped.

"So you want to play then?"

"All I have to do is tease you? Touch you? *Fuck* you?"

"And hope we get caught."

"Sounds …dangerous," he said. I thought that was the end of our conversation because he stepped away from me, deflating my heart.

"Church—"

I was silenced as he turned abruptly and pressed his hand over my mouth and shoved me against the fridge.

"You don't fucking speak, Isabella. Not when I touch you. Not when I fuck you. I'll play this game because I love Sin. If this makes him happy, I'll do it." His other hand snaked between my legs, making my knees quake.

I let out a shaky breath against his hand as he pushed through my folds and brushed against my clit, sending sparks pinging through my body.

I maintained eye contact with him as he rubbed me until I was trembling and nearly coming on his hand.

And just as quickly as he'd started, he stopped and pulled away, his fingers wet with my arousal.

"One thing to remember. I'm in fucking charge. Not you. Do up your robe. We work on my clock, not yours." He reached out and took the water I had on the counter and left the room without a backward glance.

It was all I needed though.

Dante was going to play.

And I was going to win.

SIN

"I'm happy," I said, smiling at Bells as she sat on my lap on our patio. "And I'll finish off this great day with both you and the guys happy too."

We'd agreed to spend the afternoon together. In a few hours, I'd leave with the guys to take Ashes off school grounds to set his weekly fire in the safety of a barrel. We did it every week for him. It was his reward for not burning shit down at Chapel Crest. We never missed these. It was a group celebration.

She raised a brow at me. "Oh yeah?"

I nodded and twined my fingers with hers. "Yeah. Aren't you?"

She was silent for a moment before she shrugged. "Not really."

"What can I do to change that?" I asked, running my hand up her bare thigh. The thing with Bells was she was good at playing games. Sometimes, she said things just to get me to react. I never knew what things were serious and what weren't, so I tended to react to all of them.

"You could fuck me right now," she said softly, brushing her lips along my jaw.

I let out a low chuckle. "And that'll make you happy?"

"It might."

"Ride my cock if you think it'll help." I peppered kisses along her neck. She shivered beneath my mouth as she unbuttoned my pants.

I breathed out as she pulled my hard cock from my jeans and shifted to straddle me. She was in a pretty green sundress that gave me a great view of her cleavage. And she wasn't wearing panties.

"Condom," I murmured against her lips. I'd managed to get one out of my pocket. With her lips fused to mine, she quickly sheathed my dick in the latex before sinking onto me, earning a groan from me.

She rocked back and forth on my dick as I gripped her ass, our lips wrestling in a heated frenzy as we fucked on the patio.

No one was due home for a while, so this was bliss.

"You feel so good," she said breathlessly.

"Mm." I shoved the straps of her dress down and let her breasts spill out. Immediately, I had her leaning back so I could lavish her tits, paying special care to each tanned mound with my mouth and hands as I stayed buried inside her pussy.

"You're going to make me come," she cried out, her pussy tightening around my cock.

"Then fuck me faster," I growled, nipping a nipple and making her shudder.

She rocked faster, meeting my thrusts until she was spasming around my dick, crying out my name.

I followed a moment later, groaning softly. It was in that moment of bliss though that Church walked out onto the patio.

It wasn't like I could stop blowing my load, so I rode it out. I was certain Bells hadn't even noticed him yet.

He winked at me and leaned against the railing.

With her chest heaving, she locked her focus on him. Her eyes widened as he stared us down.

It wasn't like he'd never seen me fuck in front of him before. Hell, he oftentimes was fucking a girl with me.

But I didn't want it this time. Bells was mine. I didn't want to share.

Quickly, I brought her straps back up and covered her. She didn't try to stop me as I stayed embedded in her heat.

"What are you doing home?" I grunted out as Bells continued to stare at him.

He shrugged. "Got bored. Figured I'd get high out here." He pulled out a joint and showed it to me. "Want some?"

I nodded and lifted Bells off my cock. "Yeah, give me a minute," I muttered, getting to my feet and making sure Bells was covered. She leaned against the railing too and offered me a smile that actually reached her eyes.

My heart stopped jackknifing in my chest as I realized she really was happy.

"I'll be back." I kissed her cheek and left to clean up.

I knew I could trust Church alone with her, so I did my business and grabbed a few bottles of water from the fridge before I went back to the patio to see Church and Bells staring one another down. The tension in the air was thick and had shifted completely.

"I got you a water," I said, handing it to her.

"Thanks," she murmured as Church watched her, his face expressionless.

I sighed. They must have gotten into it. It was the only way to explain the frigidness of the situation.

"I need to go," Bells said, backing away from the railing.

"What? Why?" I glanced at Church to see him lighting his joint, his attention on the lake. He didn't seem to care one way or another, which was typical of him.

"I just. . . need to. Are you coming with me?"

I blinked at her. "Bells, I told you tonight I have plans with the guys—"

"That's typical," she snapped at me. "Making shit up like that to get out of hanging out with me. You never told me you had plans. You said we were hanging out."

I glanced at Church to see him shake his head and take a hit without looking at us.

"I said we were hanging out until I left. I can't back out on the guys. This is something we do every week for Ashes. You know that.

We've done it every week for years. Every week since you and I have been together—"

"So now you're calling me crazy? A liar?" She glared at me, her bottom lip trembling.

"I-I'm not. I'm not saying that at all—"

"You are. It's me or them." She folded her arms over her chest, tears in her eyes. "Choose."

"Bells." I approached her and put my hands on her waist. "I'm not going to choose between you or them, OK? Not tonight. Ashes needs all of us. I'm not going to back out on him."

"Not even for me? Not even for our baby?"

I froze at her words. Even Church turned to look at her, a frown on his face.

"What did you just say?" I managed to rasp.

She glanced at Church then back at me. "Our baby. I-I'm pregnant."

My hands fell away from her waist as I stumbled back. "W-we're pregnant?"

She nodded. "I didn't want to tell you like this. I-I wanted to do it another way—"

"A-are you sure?" I looked at her, my heart dancing in my throat.

She stepped over to me and nodded. "Yeah. I took a test last week. It was positive."

"Fuck," Church muttered, pulling me out of my disbelief.

"Say something," she said, glancing from Church to me.

"I-I don't know what to say. I'm going to be a dad?"

"Yes."

I swallowed and reached for her. She came easily and let me draw her against my body where I hung onto her. Tears prickled my eyes. Fear rushed through me before a sense of happiness.

If we were having a baby, it meant she'd stay. She'd not abandon me or hurt me. We'd have a child to take care of. I'd have someone else who might love me.

"I'm happy," I whispered. "I'm so happy." I hugged her tightly as she clung to me.

"Then you'll stay with me tonight? I need you," she said, twisting her fingers in my shirt.

I nodded. "I'll stay tonight."

Ashes would understand. He always did.

I tilted her chin up and kissed her deeply, my heart full of wonder, my head clearing as I realized maybe things would be OK. That this was a good thing. That maybe I'd finally figured out what had been missing in my life.

The chance to love and prove I was worthy of it.

CHURCH

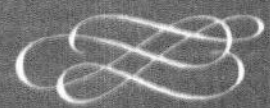

"**I** can't believe Sin got her knocked up," Stitches muttered as we leaned against the hood of my car and watched Ashes throw things into a barrel to burn.

I took a hit of my joint and passed it off to him. "I'm not surprised. She was around too much, and he was too fucking pussy-whipped to see shit clearly."

"Well, it's a bigger problem now and you know it," Stitches said, taking his hit and blowing out the smoke. "So what's the plan?"

"She's up to something," I said. "I know she is. I don't trust her."

"Me either," he muttered. "And I know Ashes doesn't, and Ashes tries to be fair about everyone."

I nodded. He was right. Ashes did try to see the good in people.

"I don't have a plan. I just need to figure out what the fuck we're going to do." I rubbed my eyes. "He loves her."

"I know. I don't see how he could. She's a bitch."

I let out a grunt. That she was.

We fell into silence as we continued to watch Ashes build an impressive fire in his metal barrel. He danced around it and whooped. His euphoria for building a fire was usually contagious, but tonight I wasn't feeling it.

Instead, I let my mind wander back to that afternoon on the patio when Sin had left to clean himself up after I'd found him fucking her.

"Did you like watching?" Isabella asked as she moved to stand beside me at the railing.

"I didn't see much." I raked my gaze over her. Her skin was still flushed from being with Sin.

She smiled up at me as she rested her hand over mine. "We're alone again. I could give you a first-hand account."

"You think I can fuck in less than five minutes?" I smirked down at her. "That's not really my style."

"You could make an exception."

"Not really in the mood."

She jutted her bottom lip out at me. "What can I do—"

"Nothing. I told you I was in charge. If it happens, it happens."

She visibly swallowed. "I want to be in charge."

"That's not how shit works with me. You should know that. You're just pussy to me. I can get that anywhere, anytime. The only reason I'm even entertaining the idea is because of Sin. Don't get your pussy wet thinking it's because of anything to do with you. My family comes first. Women come second. If I even let them."

Her nostrils flared and her cheeks darkened at my words.

"We'd be good together. Your father—"

I jerked my hand out and wrapped it tightly around her throat. "Why the fuck are you talking to me about my father? What's he got to do with any of this?"

"N-nothing. I-I just heard you were like him. I-I thought m-maybe I could help you."

I released her and shot her a sour look. "I'm nothing like him. You're more like him than I am."

She visibly swallowed. "Church, I just want you—"

"We don't always get what we want," I snapped.

She opened her mouth to answer, her dark eyes shimmering with tears that did nothing to my emotions because, seriously, fuck her.

Sin had returned only seconds later, ending the conversation. Everything I'd said was true. I wasn't interested in her at all. She was conniving and unhinged. While I enjoyed crazy, I preferred if it were me who was steering the crazy train, not some bitch trying to get some cock.

If Sin wanted to play out this little fantasy, I'd do it. No problem. No questions asked. I had been suspicious already, but once she mentioned my father that was it. I had held off on all of it before though to see how it would play out.

So far, it seemed my suspicions may be right. Something wasn't adding up.

Now this shit.

"We need to get rid of her," Stitches said.

"How if he has her knocked up?" I stared into the flames.

Stitches sighed. "I don't fucking know, but there has to be a way. What if she's not even pregnant?"

I nodded. "What if indeed. . ."

"How would we even know?"

"Aside from time?" I shook my head. "I'm not sure, but I might be able to get her away from him to free him of her chains. Not sure about the kid situation yet."

"How?" Stitches glanced at me.

"Let me take care of that. It might hurt, but I'd rather he hurt than become trapped."

We went back to watching the fire.

I needed to figure out what the deal with Sin's fantasy was. If he wasn't into it, it could be the fucking ticket to his freedom. The entire thing was just too. . . off. He'd never mentioned that shit to any of us before. If my father was involved somehow, I needed to cut the head off the fucking snake before it was too late.

Sin's fantasy was it.

It had to be my *in.*

I hated I was even contemplating it, but I'd done worse things for those I loved.

This would just be another one of them.

SIN

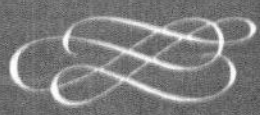

"I'm scared," I admitted softly two nights later as I held Bells in my arms in bed. "I don't know how to be a dad. My own dad tried to murder me. I-I don't exactly have good examples to use, you know?"

"My father sold me when I was three to his friends for a night of fun. My mother watched. Do you think I have a good example?" Her voice shook.

I sat up and stared down at her. She didn't speak of her past much, but I was familiar with it enough to know she'd suffered from a young age.

"Bells—"

"I don't need you to say it," she muttered. "Your pity and apologies, like it was your fault."

"I know it's not my fault. I just hurt because you hurt."

She sighed. "It is what it is. We've had a good few days. Stop trying to ruin it. You do that all the time. Things are going good, and then you decide to fucking talk about shit that no one wants to hear."

"I'm not trying to fight. I was just saying—"

"I get it," she snapped, sitting up. "Poor you. The only thing that's your fault is that you put your dick in me and got me pregnant."

"Hey, that shit's not fair. You wanted it too," I said, anger bubbling just below the surface. "Don't you blame me for any of this. *We* did this. Not just me."

"Oh, nice. Trying to pin it on me."

"Bells, I said we—"

"Just shut up, OK? All we do is fight." She rolled over and put her back to me.

I sighed and scrubbed my hand down my face. "What can I do? Do you need your meds? Water? Food?"

She stood abruptly and snatched her jeans up and began tugging them on.

"What are you doing?" I got to my feet and grabbed her wrist. She twisted it away from me before she stumbled back and fell to her ass. Tears streamed down her cheeks as I rushed to help her up. I hadn't meant for her to fall.

"You hurt me," she whispered. "You pushed me."

"I didn't push you. It was an accident. Let me help you." I made to reach for her, but she shoved me away, tears rushing down her cheeks.

"You hit me. Stop. Just stop!"

I pulled my hands away from her. "I definitely didn't hit you. What the hell is going on?"

She got to her feet and wiped at her eyes. "Leave me alone. You're always hurting me. Pushing me. Making me fuck you when I don't want to. Getting me pregnant."

My pulse roared in my ears.

"Did your meds change?" I asked softly. I had no idea why she was behaving like this and saying shit that wasn't true. "Because this isn't normal, Isabella."

"So now I'm just Isabella to you? Typical. Just used me, knocked me up, and then you abuse me."

I was really getting pissed. "What the fuck is the matter with you?" I demanded. "I love you, but I'm not going to have you saying this shit about me."

"Why? Don't want the truth to get out?" She scoffed at me, her eyes red from crying.

"That's not the truth and you know it," I said. "Come back to bed and we'll talk, OK? It's probably just stress. . . right? I love you. I'm sorry if I hurt you. I just want to talk. Come lie with me. I won't hurt you."

I was grasping at any ounce of hope to get her back in bed. She wasn't safe right then. Something was happening, and I didn't want her to be hurt because of it.

She eyed me, her bottom lip jutted out.

"Babe, come on. Come to bed. We can rest tonight. If you're still angry tomorrow, I'll let you leave, OK? I want to hold you tonight."

She stared me down for a moment before moving past me and sliding back into bed. I breathed out a sigh of relief. The fact she could flip her moods on a dime was scary. I hated it. I fucking loathed everything about it. When it was good, it was great with her. When shit was bad. . . well, it took everything I had not to completely lose my mind with her.

Every damn time she said shit to me, it dug beneath my skin, embedding itself there and making my chest ache. It put doubts in my head on whether she loved me. Wanted me. Whether I was good enough for her.

I got back into bed and held her against me.

"I love you so much," I whispered. "I want us to be OK. I'm sorry for anything I did."

She didn't say anything, but it was fine. It beat her screaming and losing it on me. Tomorrow, I'd try to get her to go into the clinic and get checked over.

For now, I'd hold her and pray I wasn't the fuck up she made me feel like I was.

✝

I WOKE up to blinding pain and Bells leaning over me.

It took all of a moment to realize she had a knife and had cut my arm with it.

"What the fuck?" I shouted, nearly falling out of bed to get away from her. She was fast and followed me, knife in hand.

"Bells," I warned. "What are you doing? Put down the knife."

"Did it hurt like you hurt me?" she demanded, her eyes flashing in the moonlight. "When you hit me earlier? When you pushed me down? You tried to hurt my baby!"

What the actual fuck was happening?

I backed away, knowing I was probably going to have to get physical to get the knife away from her and already hating myself for it.

"I'm asking you to please put the knife down. We can talk, OK?"

"No." She lunged at me and caught my arm again. The pain burned through me, but I captured her wrist and we wrestled. She was stronger than I thought she'd be, but when push came to shove, she was no match for my strength.

We crashed against my bedside table and the lamp fell to the floor, breaking on impact.

I overpowered her and the knife fell from her hand and clattered to the floor.

My bedroom door swung open and Ashes stood in the doorway, his hair a mess from sleep.

"What the fuck is going on—"

"Help me," I shouted. "Call the fucking wards. She needs help."

Ashes sprung into action and rushed from the room. A moment later, Church was at my side with Stitches as we tried to subdue Bells.

"Fucking damnit!" Stitches howled when she bit his hand. I knew it was taking all his willpower to not hit her for the action. Stitches's go-to was always violence.

It was Church who grabbed her shoulders and shook her hard. She stared up at him, her body immediately relaxing and the fight leaving.

She collapsed against his chest as Ashes came back into the room, three wards with him. The wards were basically orderlies the medical facility sent out for troubled students.

"I don't want to go," Bells mumbled as they reached down to take her from Church. She clung to him.

"You need help. You're in my fucking house, attacking people," Church hissed at her. "Go. Get some fucking help, OK?"

His words seemed to get through to her, because she let him go, allowing the wards to lift her to the gurney and strap her down.

"She'll be in holding," one of the guys grunted. "Probably until morning."

"She's pregnant," I whispered. "I-I don't know what's going on."

"Docs will look into it. Call in the morning for a status."

I nodded numbly as they took her away. I wanted to comfort her and tell her it would be OK, but she didn't want me right then.

Maybe she didn't want me at all.

She blamed me for all of this shit.

I'd had a few weeks of happiness all for it to crumble like this. And for what? I had no fucking idea what had happened. I could only assume it was stress and her mental health needed looking after.

Ashes clapped me on the back.

"It'll be OK. She needs some help," he said softly.

"Are you OK?" Church turned to me as the wards left. "You're bleeding."

I shook my head to clear it, my guts churning. "I'm fine."

"What happened?" Stitches asked as I went to my dresser and grabbed out an old t-shirt and wrapped it around the worst wound. It might need stitches, but I'd wait it out. I needed a moment to breathe and get my shit together.

I quickly told the tale of the evening, finishing with a sad sigh.

"It's not your fault. Don't think it is," Ashes assured me as I sat on my bed, the guys perched on various furniture in my room. "She had a mental break. She needs to get better."

"She won't get better here," I mumbled. "Sully is a fucking creep."

"Yeah, but she'll be medicated. Maybe she can turn her shit around on her own once she's cooled off," Stitches said. "It's happened to me a time or two."

I nodded and rubbed my eyes. "I'm sorry this shit got you guys up."

"You need to leave her," Church said, ignoring my apology. "She's turning you into something you're not. We all see it."

I scoffed. "I love her."

"She hates you," he said softly.

I swallowed and stared at my hands in my lap. The truth of the matter was, I had this nagging voice in the back of my mind that said the same thing.

"I can fix this. I fucked it up. I have to fix it. We're having a baby," I murmured. "I just. . . I can do this. I have to. I won't be a piece of shit like my old man was. I can't leave my kid."

Church let out a sigh but didn't say anything else.

"Try to get some rest," Ashes said. "It's a worry for another day."

I nodded as Church left the room without another word. I knew he was upset. He tended to get that way when one of us didn't listen to him. He just needed to understand. . . fuck. Maybe I needed to understand. My head was a confused fucking mess.

My heart was worse.

"Man. . . this is why chicks suck," Stitches grumbled. "Should have gotten him a fucking fish."

I let out a huff of sad laughter and crawled back into bed, not giving a shit about the cuts on my arm.

I just wanted to sleep forever. It hurt too much to think that maybe Church was right. What sort of person would take a knife to you while you slept if they loved you? It made me sick to my stomach. I'd thought my father had loved me too, but he'd shot me in the chest.

Maybe I didn't even know what the fuck love was.

Maybe I wasn't destined for it.

I didn't want to feel sorry for myself, but everything in my life pointed to maybe I really was the problem in the fucking equation.

Stitches bid me good night and left the room while Ashes sat on the edge of my bed.

"Don't get caught up in your head, man," he whispered into the darkness. "Just don't. It won't lead you anywhere good."

"I know," I answered back softly.

"Just sleep. We can talk tomorrow. Things will be better then."

I swallowed hard and didn't say anything.

Ashes got to his feet and left the room, leaving me to my thoughts.

To my pain.

To my guilt.

When the cards were all out on the table, all this shit was my fault. I'd gotten her pregnant. I knew that day I shouldn't have fucked her without anything. But fuck.

I wept softly into my pillow, wondering if I'd ever get shit right.

CHURCH

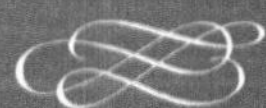

Something was up.

I stared back at Isabella as she sat at her table, eating alone. Sin had gone to her the following morning after she'd attacked him and had sat with her all day. That was a week ago. Now, all they did was fucking fight. Sin was currently in a therapy session, but I expected he'd be arriving shortly to argue with her some more.

"She needs to go," Stitches said, following my gaze.

"I don't disagree," I murmured, taking in the way she offered me a sexy smile. She ducked her head quickly, like she was some shy sweetheart. I knew she was a fucking pit viper though.

"Sin won't let her go though. All the shit she's put him through and he keeps going back," Stitches continued.

I looked over at him and nodded. I hadn't said a word to anyone about what had happened in our kitchen with her. And it wasn't because I was scared or shit like that. I was playing a game, after all, and that was one of my favorite things to do.

"We're all gluttons for punishment one way or another," I said.

Stitches grumbled and bit into his pizza and went silent. I continued to watch Isabella, knowing that if I wanted to get her away from Sin, I'd have to make a move. A move that was really going to hurt Sin if my suspicions were true. I'd been rolling it over in my mind since the kitchen incident with her.

Sometimes to save someone you had to hurt them. The pain may change him, but in the end, if something didn't get done, he was going to fall even harder. I had to trade one evil for another.

It was the story of my fucking life.

✝

A WEEK LATER, I watched as Sin sat staring at a wall in the living room. He had a cut on his chin and bruises littered his jaw. He hadn't spoken since he'd gotten home over an hour ago from seeing Isabella, but it didn't take a genius to figure out they'd been fighting again.

Stitches shot me a quick look, his dark brows crinkled. We were all thinking the same thing. That bitch needed to go.

"Sin?" Ashes called out, glancing at me. "You want to talk about it?"

"No," he grunted, lifting his bottled water to his lips and taking a sip.

"Dude, break up with her. You can still take care of your kid if you're not together," Stitches said. "You're a fucking mess, man. Your face is fucked."

"It was just a bad day," he murmured, not bothering to look away from the wall. "That's all. Tomorrow will be better."

Sin was checking the fuck out on us. He wasn't this guy. The Sinclair Priest I knew was filled with fury and didn't take shit from anyone. He'd fought his way out of everything in his life and emerged on the other side.

I'd be damned if I let this bitch take him out when bullets couldn't.

Without a word, I got to my feet and left the room. I didn't want to hurt him, god I didn't, but all was fair in love and war and this bitch chose the wrong guy to go to war with.

No one fucked with my friends, my brothers, and got away with it. Pussy or not, we were all equals here.

If she wanted to play, we'd fucking play.

SIN

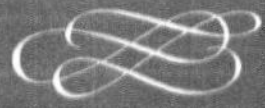

I bit back a hiss as Bells's nails gouged my neck. My tolerance was waning lately. I wanted to be supportive of her break or whatever the fuck was happening, but this shit was getting painful in more ways than one. She made me bleed daily. She screamed at me. Then she'd hold me and kiss me and tell me how sorry she was.

But then it would happen again.

It was brutal, and it was fucking up everything.

"Bells, come on," I coaxed, wrapping my arms around her small frame as she snarled obscenities at me for probably the tenth time that day. "Relax. Let's just relax. Together."

"Fuck you," she snapped. "Let me go. You're always doing this to me! You're always hurting me! Let me go! Let me fucking go! All you do is ruin everything. Everything you touch, Sinclair! You're ruining me! I want to be alone and you just can't let it happen!"

I released her, my chest heaving. I was so tired of dealing with it. Shame washed through me daily over my feelings of just wanting to walk away. If I couldn't handle her hateful words and outbursts, how the hell was I ever going to make it through her pregnancy and be there for the baby? It was driving me to the edge of what little sanity I had left.

"Fine," I shouted, losing it as she glared at me, her lips twisted into a sneer. There was nothing on her face that suggested she gave a shit for me in that moment. Maybe I'd been trying too hard. Clinging too tightly when I needed to let her have space.

"You want me to leave you alone? Then I will. Don't fucking hurt yourself or the baby," I continued, trying to keep my voice even.

She rolled her eyes at me. "There you go again. Accusing me—"

"I'm not fucking accusing you of anything. I'm just telling you to be safe. That's all." I backed to the door of her dorm. "Just. . . please. I'll give you space. I love you. So fucking much. I only want you to be safe."

She continued to glare at me until I turned and left the room, blood on my neck and face from her latest attack. She said her meds had changed. I wanted to believe it, and I'm sure they had changed, but I couldn't attribute it all to that. As long as I'd known her, she'd been a little volatile. I accepted that. Even thought I might be able to fix her.

But fuck.

At what cost?

I needed to fucking breathe.

I walked back to the house and smoked a joint, letting the high wash through me. It was too early in the day for me to spend it blitzed the fuck out, but I needed an escape. I had another class soon, so once I finished smoking, I left.

"Hey," Ashes called out to me as I walked through the outdoor commons minutes later after coming back from the house.

"Hey," I muttered.

"You're bleeding," he said, falling in step with me. "Bells?"

I nodded wordlessly.

"You can't keep doing this." He sighed. "I'm worried."

"Me too." I stopped and turned to him. "I don't know what to do, man. I love her. We're having a kid. She's just driving me fucking nuts though. Makes me feel like I'm a complete fuck up. I try to make things right. . ." I sighed and rubbed my eyes. I was fucking clueless at this point.

"Maybe it's time to accept the relationship has run its course."

"How is that possible when I got her pregnant?"

Ashes gave me a sad look. "You can still take care of your kid. It doesn't mean you have to stick it out with her. For fuck's sake, man, you're bleeding. You're going to have a hell of a scar on your arm and probably even other parts of your body. That's not love. That's assault, brother."

I exhaled. "I know. I just. . . fuck, man. What do I do?"

"Talk to her. You need peace. No one should have to live like that. She's telling you how she feels with every fight and every attack."

"Maybe it's a cry for help," I said sadly, hating the pain his words brought me.

"Or maybe she's *really* telling you, Sin." He reached out and clapped me on the shoulder. "You're not alone. Never think you are. We're here for you. Always. You know that, right?"

"I know," I mumbled, looking to the sky. It was growing dark as clouds gathered. I'd heard there was supposed to be a storm this evening. I loved when it stormed. I'd sit and stare out at the lake, watching the waves batter the shore. It matched my mood perfectly today.

"I gotta go, but think about it, OK?" Ashes said, backing away. "You need the peace. Believe me. We all do."

"I know," I said softly.

He gave me a nod and left. I turned and caught Asylum's eye. He'd been watching me from a stone bench. He cocked his head at me, his face emotionless.

I broke contact with him, chills rushing through my body. He had a way of putting me on edge. The last thing I felt like dealing with today was him, so I turned and made my way into the school, promising myself I'd figure out a solution by the time classes ended for the day.

That solution would include me figuring out how to give Bells the love she deserved. The sort of love we could both live with because if her misery was anything like my own, then heaven have mercy on our souls.

The only thing I wanted was happiness. If I had to sacrifice my own for hers, I'd do it. I knew I would. I just fucking loved her. That's all I knew. But I had to love me too. I knew that much. But how the hell do you love a monster whose own parents didn't want him?

Maybe that was the problem the entire time. Not her.

Maybe it was me.

Feeling even more glum, I went to classes, a lead weight on my heart.

Tonight. We'll figure it out tonight.

It was the best comfort I could tell myself.

I was pretty sure I was a damn liar though.

BELLS

I calmed down enough by the end of the day that I'd decided it was time to talk to Sin. I had no idea what I was going to tell him. Maybe apologize and keep trying to get closer to Church. At the root of it all, I was sure all my anger was stemming from not having gotten Church yet. I'd been so close a few times, but he always pushed me away.

In that respect, he wasn't like Everett. Well, maybe a little since Everett had told me not to return until I had his son under my thumb as he'd buried himself in my ass, his cock wrecking me to tears.

It was late. I was sure Sin would be home by now. I hadn't bothered to text or call him. He'd only sent one text.

I love you, Bells.

It had made me grind my teeth.

Why couldn't Church just tell me that? I saw the way he kept looking at me. I knew he wanted me.

I sighed, pushing the thoughts out of my head. All they did was put me on edge and make me angry and desperate. And violent. Too violent as of late.

I knocked on the front door to the watchers' house and waited. A moment later, Church opened the door.

"H-hey," I said, surprised he was there.

"Isabella," he murmured, his green eyes sweeping over me. My heart jumped in my chest as his deep voice tickled my senses. "Come in."

He stepped aside for me and I entered the house, him closing the door after me.

"I suspect you're feeling better?" He was still focused on me.

I nodded. "Yes. Lots."

He surveyed me. "Good. Because Sin's not here. Ashes and Stitches took him out for a bit."

My heart leaped. "It's just us?"

His eyes roved up my body. "It's just us."

I took that as the invite I'd been dreaming about. I wasted no time as I closed the distance between us. The moment I reached him, I placed my hand on his chest.

"Can I touch you?" I whispered, my heart in my throat.

"No. I touch you. That's how this works."

I swallowed thickly and nodded. I was game for whatever he wanted. I couldn't believe my luck. I knew we were meant to be.

I said as much as he wrapped his hand over mine and led me into the living room.

"We're destined," I said.

He grunted and said nothing as he released my hand. "Take off your clothes."

I didn't hesitate or consider anything past my desperation for him. I simply unzipped the dress I was wearing and let it fall to the floor before I removed my bra and pushed my panties down.

I stood naked before the man I was destined for, watching as his eyes trailed over my body.

"Do you like what you see?" I asked.

"It'll do."

I jutted out my bottom lip. "You don't think I'm sexy?"

"I think you're a piece of ass willing to do whatever I want. That's all that's important."

I frowned deeper at that. He was supposed to love me.

A look I didn't recognize flitted over his handsome face as I stared back at him. It was a look I'd never seen on him before. Maybe it was. . . sadness?

No, that couldn't be right.

I leaned in to kiss him, my breasts brushing against his t-shirt. He jerked away from me before my lips found their destination.

"I don't kiss," he growled, his eyes flashing.

"Not even me?"

"*Especially* you."

I bit my bottom lip. He was a lot harder to figure out than I thought he was going to be. I assumed he was just playing hard to get, so I reached out and pressed my hand to the front of his pants to find him not hard.

I went to my knees and stared up at him. He didn't say a word to me, so I unbuttoned his pants and pulled his zipper down, my heartbeat thundering in my ears.

This was it. The moment I'd yearned for.

I pulled his length out and stroked him, hoping he'd get hard for me. I wasn't disappointed. His cock sprung to life, so thick and long.

So beautiful. So perfect. So. . . mine.

I didn't like to give head. I never even tried to do a good job when I did it. Swallowing was out of the question too, but with Church I wanted to do everything in my power to make him desperate to have me like I was desperate to have him.

I licked the head of his cock, tasting the bead of saltiness at the tip.

Still, he remained silent, his eyes trained on me. Deciding it was time to get what I yearned for, I parted my lips and slid his cock deep into my mouth and sucked.

He grunted slightly before tangling his fingers in my hair and helping to move me along his length.

He was gentle at first until he grew rougher, forcing my mouth deeper onto his dick, choking me. My nails dug into his thighs as I took all he had to give me, which was saying something because Dante Church was packing some serious heat.

He picked up his pace and fucked my mouth mercilessly.

I cried out against his cock as he reached out and slapped my face.

"Deeper. You're doing terrible," he snarled.

I breathed out, trembling. I was trying really hard to please him. I took him deeper, gagging on his dick as he hit the back of my throat.

He let out a wicked little laugh and forced his way deeper into my throat.

"You're just a stupid little bitch, aren't you?" he asked. "Can't even suck cock right. No wonder Sin is so miserable. Useless. That's what you are."

Tears prickled my eyes at his words.

"You going to cry for me, Isabella? Huh? Real bad ass on the outside, but words hurt you, don't they? You're rotten and worthless. Can't even suck cock good enough to get me off. Is your pussy as bad as your mouth?" He tugged his cock from my mouth and shoved me to the floor. I landed on my hands and knees with a soft whimper.

"Let's see how sloppy this pussy is. Heard you've had a lot of cock in it." He lined up behind me on his knees and shoved his dick through my folds without further fanfare.

I cried out as he breached me. I hadn't heard him unwrap a condom and put it on, but I could feel that he was wearing one.

My heart sank. I'd wanted to feel his hot flesh inside my body. I'd wanted to carry his seed inside me and feel it dribble down my thighs as I walked back to my room. Using his come as lube as I lay in bed later and touched myself to my memory of him.

He sank deep into my heat with a soft grunt, his hands tight on my hips.

"Oh my god. Fuck," I gasped.

He said nothing as he pulled out and shoved his way back into my pussy. Over and over again, his breathing growing heavier with each powerful thrust into my body.

I reached down and rubbed my clit, knowing I wasn't going to need it because he was fucking his way to my sweet spot without even trying.

"Fuck. Church. Feels so good," I called out breathlessly as I rubbed my clit in time to his fucking.

He fucked me harder. Faster. His hips snapped hard against my bare asscheeks as he railed into my heat so fast I thought he was going to build a fire from the friction. The sound of our heavy breathing and slapping skin sounded out in the otherwise silent room.

"I-I'm going to come. Please. Please, don't stop. Don't!" I shouted, my release just at the surface. I fell forward, my body trembling as Church slowed his pace.

"No," I moaned. "Faster. More. D-Don't slow down."

My pleasure began to recede as Church continued to slow.

It took me a moment to register the door had opened and someone was calling my name.

I lifted my head and looked up to see Sin standing in the middle of the room, his mouth open.

Church immediately pulled free of my body, not having finished either.

"What the fuck?" Sin shouted, blinking rapidly.

I sighed, pissed off that Sin had once again ruined everything, and grabbed my dress as Church pulled the empty condom off and threw it at me. It landed on my bare chest and he gave me a sneer as he tucked his dick away.

"Are you fucking kidding?" Sin continued, his voice raising. "Are you *FUCKING* kidding me?" His breath caught as I pulled my dress on, not bothering with my bra or panties. Church could have those as his little trophy for claiming my pussy.

"Church, man? H-how could you?" Sin's voice cracked and broke as Stitches and Ashes walked in. They looked at the scene, clearly understanding what had happened.

Sin launched himself forward to attack Church, but Stitches was quick to dart in front of him and shove him back at Ashes who grabbed his arms as Sin fought against them.

"How could you? You're my best friend! How could you fucking do this to me?" Sin wailed, sobbing. The fight left him and he sagged against Stitches who had moved forward.

"Easy, man," Stitches murmured.

"She told me you wanted this," Church called out. "Said it was your fantasy to walk in on it."

"Fuck. . . fucking never," Sin rasped, his body trembling. He pulled away from Stitches a moment later, Ashes having released his arms.

"I never wanted that. Bells. . . how could you do this to me? You know how much I love you. Why would you do this? And with my friend? I-I don't understand."

"Because I fucking *hate* you, Sinclair," I snarled, balling my hands into fists. "All you've done since I've met you is ruin my life. Even tonight, you fucking ruined it! You won't let me have a damn thing, not even my freedom since you got me pregnant with a fucking baby I didn't even want. I hate this fucking baby! I hate you! Fuck you! I hope you fucking shatter into a million pieces that you'll never be able to pick up because you don't deserve to be whole! You're a worthless prick. You're trash. Even your parents didn't want you. No one is ever going to love you! NO ONE! I know I never will!" I stormed past him as he remained silent, tears streaming down his face.

I stopped at the door amid the silence and turned around.

"Church," I called out.

"Go fuck yourself," he answered softly.

I swallowed hard, hesitating for a moment before I pulled the door open and stepped into the night, only one regret alive within me.

And that was the fact I hadn't gotten to tell Church how much I loved him.

That was fine. He knew what he'd be missing now. I'd seen the look in his eyes. I felt how he moved inside me. He wanted me. He just couldn't come out and say it yet.

I needed to tell Everett how good a job I'd done with Church. How he wouldn't be able to live without me now.

I smiled as I stepped off the front stairs from the watchers' house.

Life was really looking up.

SIN

"We need to talk," Church said softly three days after I'd found him balls deep inside my girlfriend.

"Fuck you," I muttered as I smoked a joint and stared out at the lake. I hadn't spoken a word to him. After Bells had left that night, I'd gone to my room and curled up into a tight ball on my bed and cried like a little bitch until I'd fallen asleep.

He'd betrayed me. He was my best friend and he'd fucked my girl behind my back. I knew Church liked women, but I never thought he'd do that to me. Was I surprised? Not really, at least when it came to Bells's part in all of it. I knew she liked him. I hadn't wanted to admit it, but I fucking knew.

"Come on," Church said. "Enough of this shit. I let you pout it out for a few days. It's time we sort through shit."

"Easy," Ashes called out. "No fighting."

I turned and looked at Church. "I have nothing to say to you. We're not friends. We're not brothers. In fact, if Ashes set you on fire right now, I wouldn't waste a drop of piss to put you out."

Church rolled his eyes at me. "You're being dramatic. Come on. Enough."

I scoffed at him. "She was my girl. The mother to my child—"

"If it's even yours," Church snapped. "She's a fucking whore. You know she is. Why do you even think she's only been fucking you? For all you know, even Danny Linley has probably had his tiny pecker up in her sloppy pussy."

"Man, fuck you!" I pushed off the railing to the patio and shoved him hard in the chest. He took a step back, his eyes flashing.

"Watch yourself," he growled. "I didn't do this *to* you. I did it *for* you."

I let out a bark of bitter laughter as Stitches rushed outside and Ashes stepped closer. I knew they'd end a fight before we even got started, but fuck it. I'd still give it a go.

"You're a real fucking piece of shit, Church. I trusted you! I fucking trusted you. And this is how you repay me? I've always been there for you. For you to fuck my girl who is pregnant with my kid just fucking disgusts me! I don't even have words for any of this shit. It's just unbelievable. You're fucking dead to me. You hear me? Dead."

"You have your head so far up that bitch's pussy, you're blind," Church shot back. "She doesn't want you. She even told you she hates you. Why can't you see what she was doing? She was playing a fucking game with you."

I shook my head at him. "So why'd you do it then? Huh? If you knew she was playing a game. Why'd you fuck her? Why'd you fuck my girl?" My anger was getting the better of me. I took a step forward, but Stitches was right there to push me back as he got between me and Church. I knew if push came to shove, Ashes and Stitches would fight me and Church to keep us separated.

"I did it to fucking save you," he called out. "You're just too pussy-whipped yet to see it. She was using you. She wanted me! You were just a fucking stepping stone for her—"

I didn't even let him finish the sentence. I launched myself forward and knocked Stitches to the side as Ashes tried to intervene. My fist collided with Church's jaw in a sickening, satisfying crack before all hell broke loose.

No one hit Dante Church and got away with it.

Within moments, we were beating on one another, both of us snarling obscenities and bleeding from our heavy hits on one another.

"Stop! Fucking stop!" Ashes shouted as he and Stitches tried to tug us apart.

Briefly, we were torn apart only for me to launch myself at Church again.

Stitches's fist met my jaw in a hit so hard I saw stars and stumbled back. Stitches knew how to fight. He was violent by nature, and once he was pissed off, there was no caging the animal he became.

He lunged at me and took me to the ground. We rolled around, punching one another before we were tugged apart.

"We're not fucking doing this! We're not!" Stitches yelled as Church held him back and Ashes tugged me away. "You're my brothers. I'm not fucking doing this! It's gone on enough. Sin, Isabella is a fucking cunt, plain and simple. The fact you're OK with all the shit she's done is what's disgusting. I don't know why the fuck Church did what he did, but I'm out. I'm not fucking putting up with it. Me and Ashes aren't interested in this shit. It's over. You and Isabella *are over*. Let that bitch go. She doesn't want you. She did you a favor. So did Church. Take it and fucking move on!" His chest heaved as he stared at me. "We're family, man."

"He's no family of mine." I spit at him. "He's dead to me."

Church glared at me, but he didn't say anything as I jerked free from Ashes and stormed into the house. When I got to my bedroom, I slammed my door closed.

Everything was falling apart.

Fuck it all.

✝

IT TOOK me the rest of the night to calm down. What Bells had done had shredded my heart. She was right. She'd shattered me. I had no clue why she hated me the way she did. All I ever did was love her.

115

And the baby.

Fuck.

What about the baby?

I wanted answers. I deserved them.

Or did I?

I didn't know what the hell I deserved anymore. Maybe all of this. Who the hell knew.

I picked up my phone and stared down at her name on the screen. Hesitating for only a moment, I finally called her, listening as her phone rang. She'd left campus. That much I knew. Her guardian had come and picked her up yesterday. I didn't even know who the hell her guardian was. She never talked about him. I just knew she had one. A male. That was all the information I had on the subject.

I hung up and dialed again. It went to her voicemail.

I cleared my throat. "Bells. Hey, it's me. I-I just want to know what I did to deserve all this shit? Was I that awful to you? I-I don't know what to do. The baby. . ." my voice shook and cracked. "Please. Whatever you do, just take care of our baby. Please. I-I know you're having second thoughts. I miss you. Fuck, I hate that I do. And I love you." I sniffled, hating myself for being so weak. "I just want to make sure you're OK. Please. Even just a text letting me know you're safe. That the baby is fine. You have a doctor's appointment next week. Please don't forget. Please go to it and take care of the baby. And yourself. I'm sorry for everything. If you come back. . ."

I wiped at my eyes.

"Text me. Call me. Doesn't matter what time. I love you, Bells. I'm so sorry for everything. I-I'm sorry." I disconnected the call and laid back in bed, hating that I was fucking crying again.

When I'd woken in the hospital after I'd survived the attempted murder and suicide from my father, my first thought had been *what did I do?*

That same question rolled through my mind now. I've spent years wondering what I'd done wrong for my father to put that bullet through my chest and try to kill me. I'd never found the answer to that question. In therapy, they told me it wasn't me. It was him. It was his sickness, not mine. I didn't believe that for a moment. There was just something about me people hated. Even my mother tossed me aside when I'd needed her most. She said I was scaring her. That I scared her twerp of a husband she'd married. That I needed help.

I had needed help.

I'd needed her help, and she abandoned me.

Bells left me too.

Why? Fucking why?

Because I wasn't worthy. It was the only answer I had. Bells was right. I was worthless. Useless. Something to be tossed aside when something better came along.

I sniffled and wiped at my eyes.

Whatever.

It didn't fucking matter anymore. I knew Bells was different. I just didn't think she'd do this to me. She had me fooled. Or maybe I had myself fooled.

Either way, I'd been played. Hard.

It fucking sucked.

I breathed out and focused on my feelings as I let them out to breed in my heart.

Hatred.

My love was turning to hatred.

The feeling ignited slowly within me, making me wince.

I exhaled again.

I needed to sleep.

My eyes closed as I steadied my anger and everything that came with it.

I'd explore it another time. Right now, it was all too raw and painful. I'd never be able to think clearly if I was hurting this much.

But hell, maybe I was thinking clearly. Everything she'd said about me was true.

I had a history of examples to look at.

"I'm sorry," I whispered into the darkness of my room. "For whatever I've done, God, I'm sorry. Please. . . I don't want to be punished any longer. Please, God. I'm begging you. Save me. Please fucking save me. I just want to be normal. I want to be loved by someone I can love back. I want to be free of this pain. Please. Fucking please help me."

I repeated my prayer until sleep took me.

And even in my dreams, I said it.

But that was simply just a nightmare because in it, Bells was laughing at me for being so fucking stupid.

CHURCH

*I*t wasn't often that I was miserable at Chapel Crest. Yes, I hated it there, but it was my sanctuary away from the madness I'd endured growing up. It was my haven. My place of solace. My place of power.

Now, I was powerless as I watched Sin crumble and break.

Bells had really fucked him up.

I'd helped, so I was no angel, but I'd done it to save him, not hurt him. I knew if I fucked her, he'd lose it and let her go.

Of course, that meant I ran the risk of losing him as well, but if it meant he was away from her conniving ass, I was willing to risk it.

I hadn't even gotten off on her pussy. I'd felt nothing as I'd fucked her.

She was a means to an end. That's all.

"Mr. Church, you're wanted in the office," Sister Helen called out as I sat in her Bible study class.

Normally, I'd tell her and whoever was beckoning me to the office to fuck off, but in this instance, I needed the distraction from my fucked up thoughts. I gathered my stuff and made my way to the office at the center of the campus and went inside.

I stopped in my tracks as my father walked out of Sully's office, that shitty, wicked smile on his face.

"What do you want?" I demanded. I hated my father. To my very fucking soul, I hated that man. He was wicked and twisted and a million shades of fucked up. His sole purpose in life was to try to make me just like him.

He succeeded in many ways, but failed in so many more.

"Dante. My son," he greeted me, the glint in his eyes not affection, but wickedness.

"What do you want?" I repeated in a low voice.

I glanced at Sully to see a matching smile on that prick. My father paid him off to fuck shit up around here. I was almost sure of it. Wicked men tended to stick together.

"Dante, your father was just telling me how you're going to tour the Mayfair campus next summer. That's exciting. Mayfair is a top university. Only the very best, brightest, and. . . *sane* make it in there." Sully winked at me.

Fuckhead cunt.

"Or those with enough money to buy their way in," I said evenly. "I'm sure I'll manage if I decide to attend."

My father chuckled, nothing in the motion showcasing actual humor. It was all a display. He was like a peacock strutting around, showing off.

"Well, winning is winning, no matter how we do it, right?" Sully chuckled.

I wanted to punch him in the throat but refrained and focused on my father. "Are you going to answer me? What are you doing here?"

"Can't a father come visit his son?" Father let out a soft laugh.

"I'll leave you two to it. Everett, always a pleasure." Sully shook his hand and returned to his office, leaving us alone in the waiting area. Even the old bitch behind the desk had left to give us privacy.

"Let's talk." Father nodded for me to follow him. Sighing, I did, knowing the sooner we spoke, the sooner he'd be out of there.

I walked beside in him in silence until we made it to the old cemetery on the edge of the school grounds.

One of my favorite places in the world.

Probably because the dead didn't have shit to say.

We sat on a stone bench beneath a willow that I often sat at during my adventures into the forest. I loved that bench. It was my thinking spot.

I hated that he was tarnishing it with his ass.

"I've missed you," he started.

"Lies. You don't miss shit," I shot back.

He chuckled. "Always so witty, Dante. Like your mother."

"You don't talk about her." Anger rushed to the surface at the mention of my mother who had long since passed. She was a prisoner to him like I was. At least she was free now. More than I could say for myself.

"Right. I forgot our agreement." His lips twitched. "The weather is nice, don't you think?"

It took everything I had not to lose it and plant my fist in the center of his face.

"Why are you really here? I know it's not to talk about the weather."

"I was wondering where you stand on joining me. You weren't overly helpful this summer. Given your love of murdering small animals, I thought humans would help quench your thirst."

"Only some humans." I glared at him. If it fazed him, he didn't show it.

He laughed at that.

"Ah, I feel that way sometimes too, but you know me. I enjoy what I do."

I said nothing, letting him have whatever fucking moment he was having with himself.

"I came to you today because I wanted to know when I can expect you to join me in our empire. You're getting to that age where I need you. You're my legacy, Dante. Together, we could be feared through the underground."

"We're already feared."

"Yes, but not together. Imagine the power we'd wield if you'd just agree to come home."

"I'm not interested in the family business. I've told you this before."

His cheerful mood dissipated. "How can you not be? You were born and raised in blood and screams."

I shook my head at him. "And look at me now. Violent. Twisted. I struggle with controlling my murdering urges. It's no way to live, Father."

"It's the perfect way to live once you let go and fucking own who you are."

"I'm not interested. I don't feel anything, and I like it like that. I like where I am."

"Yes, I've heard all about it," he said, glaring at me. "*Isabella.*"

"I'm sure you have," I murmured. "Since you seem to have her crazy ass in your pocket too."

He let out a huff of laughter that oozed his darkness. "She wasn't supposed to tell you."

"She's a bit of an idiot. To be fair, she didn't come out and say it, but your name came up a time or two. I put two and two together. Honestly, Father. I expected better from you. A teen girl? Really?"

"She's hot pussy, Dante. And you're a young man that I assume loves to bury himself in pussy. Aren't you? Or do you like cock?"

I clenched my teeth and gathered my cool. "What do you care what I like? You only want me for one thing."

"I'd want you for two if I thought you wouldn't cry on me. You and your mother seemed to get along rather well—"

"Shut the fuck up," I snarled. "You know it wasn't like that with her. You know what you did—"

"And I know what I saw, son. *I know.*" He stared me down. "Are you coming home or not?"

"Not now. Not fucking ever."

"At some point, you won't have a choice."

"And when that day comes, Father, I assure you it will be *because* I've made a choice. Go fuck your teen whore. I'm not interested in whatever shitty plot you're working on."

"*Shitty plot*," he mused. "I promised you to her. If she brought you home. She said you fucked her. Her pussy isn't the best. I suppose that's because it's been used for so long."

I scoffed, hating the prick even more. I knew something was up, and I was right. Of course he'd had his hands deep in the pot. The fact he'd done all of this and had created issues within my group really pissed me off.

I made a silent vow right then and there that someday I'd kill the fucker and piss on his corpse for all the inconveniences he'd put in my life. For all the moments like these.

"How do you even know her?" I asked, needing some confirmation on my thoughts.

"She's your sister." He got to his feet and smiled down at me. "I adopted her and kept her in the dungeon. She's not blood, but she works hard. She's been helping me train the kids. I let her play with them sometimes. I enjoy seeing her get close to them. She snaps sometimes though. She killed one last night. I put her in the room with the pretty little girl we acquired days before. Just a child. I told her she could have fun and do what she needed to do to let her anger out. A test, really."

I steadied myself, maintaining my emotionless demeanor to him.

"She made that little girl her friend. Then. . . she stomped on her head until she stopped crying. Bloody mess." He chuckled. "Too bad. She'd have fetched a lot of money. Little blue-eyed, blonde hair girls often do."

"Bells killed the girl?"

"Oh yes. Then. . . well, we had a little fun. I do like celebrations." He looked to the sun streaming in through the top of the willow. "Dinner was spectacular, Dante. So tender and sweet. You'd have loved it."

"I very much doubt that," I snarled.

"As if you've never feasted before."

I glared at him.

"I suppose we'll try again later. Perhaps you're still too young and naive. We have a few years. I was just being optimistic. Tell Sinclair I send my love. And Stitches too. You know he's a back-up plan in case you fail to see reason." He inclined his head at me. "Perhaps when Bells returns, she can help me train Sinclair. His madness would be perfect in the business once he breaks. I'm sure she did a fantastic job with him."

I said nothing as he smiled at me.

"I'll be seeing you. I have another to see here before I leave today. He's going to give you a run for your money, or so he tells me." He laughed.

I still didn't react. I wanted him gone. Any reaction from me would have made him happy. I'd give the prick nothing.

I didn't even care who the fuck he had to see. It could have all just been him fucking with my head. He was a deviant prick like that.

He walked away, whistling as he went, leaving me alone beneath the willow.

If I had my way, I'd kill him now, but I knew I had to bide my time.

Good things came to those who waited.

I was fucking betting on it.

And Bells. . . that bitch would get hers. I just needed some time to get some things sorted out before I made my final play.

After all, I wasn't new to the game I played with my father.

I'd ante up if it's what he wanted.

BELLS

"Everett?" I called out as I poked my head into his office. Everett was my guardian. He'd taken me after killing my father years ago. He'd given me a *taste* of revenge in more ways than one. He never let me stay in his home though. He swore me to secrecy. Church was never to know that I was his adopted sister. Same for Stitches.

He kept me at his office, in a dungeon in the basement. It was a decent set-up. He didn't let the men touch me like he did other girls he kept. Or boys. Instead, he took care of me and made me feel so good. He taught me how to hurt people. How to win. How to fuck.

I did all the things he asked of me. I lured in the children for him. The young girls. Even the boys. Sometimes, when I was really good, he'd let me watch while they were hurt by the men. While they screamed and begged for help as the monsters that dwelled these parts of the world took what they wanted.

I enjoyed it because it meant someone else got to hurt besides me.

I appreciated their pain. Demanded it. It was my freedom to watch them scream and beg. I'd fucking earned it.

"What are you doing up here?" Everett demanded without looking at me from where he sat in his dimly lit office. The fireplace crackled, warming the room.

I went to him and kneeled at his feet.

His gaze dragged over my face. He looked a lot like Church, except Everett smiled more than Church did.

"I missed you. You haven't come to see me. Where were you?"

He reached out and caressed my cheek. "Why do you think you have a right to know?"

"Because. . . I-I love you."

He moved his hand from my face, leaving cold in his wake.

"I was seeing your brother."

"Church," I whispered, my heart leaping. "Did you tell him? About everything? Me and him?"

"In a way," he said, turning his attention back to the flames.

"Was he happy?"

He said nothing as he continued to stare at the dancing fire. Worry grew deep in my belly.

"Daddy?" I asked softly.

Everett snapped his attention to me. He loved when I called him Daddy.

"You had one job, Isabella. One," he said softly, his voice sending chills over my body. "It was the easiest job, and you still failed."

"I-I didn't fail. He loves me! He fucked me!" I stared wide-eyed at him. "Sin came in and ruined everything! If he wouldn't have gotten home early, I'd have Church here with me now! I know I would have."

Everett turned away from me and stared back at the fire. My throat ached with worry as the minutes ticked by.

"You're useless, Isabella," he murmured.

"What? I-I'm not. I did a good job," I choked out, the floodgates opening and tears rushing down my cheeks. "I got Church to give in. I know I could do it again—"

"*One fucking job.* Bring my son home. I thought he was young and dumb and would fuck his way here, but you proved worthless in that endeavor."

"I-I can do it. I swear I can. I'll go back—"

"And now you're knocked up." He gave me a disgusted look. "The moment the baby is born, you will hand it over to me. I've already got buyers lined up."

"The flesh market?" I whispered, my voice trembling. "To be served on a platter?"

He scoffed. "It's on any market. Whoever pays the most gets to do whatever they want. Dine. Raise. Harvest. I care not. It's your punishment for failing me."

I got to my feet. "I don't really care about a fucking baby. I already hate it. I hate *him* for putting it in me."

"It takes two to tango, my dear Isabel. You know that." He looked away from me as I stared down at him, not quite sure what I could say to him to get him to see that I was worth it. That I could fix this.

"You're banished from my sight. I will remain your guardian until you're eighteen, and then you will return here and give yourself to the men who want you. . . for whatever they want you for."

"No. No! Daddy. . . please. I'm sorry. I'm sorry! I'll make it right. I swear! Don't do this to me. I don't have anyone else! Please! I don't want to be alone. You promised! You promised me! Please," I sobbed, reaching for him.

He got to his feet and loomed over me for a moment as I cried. His lips brushed against mine for a brief second before he stepped back.

"We're done here."

"No! No!" I wailed, reaching for him.

I had no idea when the man had arrived, but he pulled me away from Everett as I cried out for him to not do this to me.

Everett turned his back on me and went back to staring into the fire as the man dragged me from the room.

When we made it out to the hall, I sagged against him, breathing hard.

"Anson," I choked out as I stared up at him.

"At least you got out," he said softly, his blue eyes filled with emotion. Anson wasn't around much anymore. Rumor had it he'd been accepted at Mayfair and had left this life. A runner. An enforcer for Everett. A kid who was living on the streets after his mother and sister were murdered. What he was doing in Detroit was beyond me since his stomping grounds were the underground world in Chicago where Everett ran a lot of his business from. It didn't matter though. Anson always popped up when least expected.

Everett loved Anson.

I knew he did.

He loved him like he'd loved me.

Anson wasn't that type of guy though. Anson never gave in. He simply did his job and left to live his life. Everett let him because he loved him. I knew this. Anson was beautiful. Black hair. Blue eyes. Tall. Muscles. Smart. And he sang. I'd heard him. His voice was like an angel's, or what I'd assume an angel would sound like if I'd ever heard one.

"I'm not leaving. I-I can't—"

"You'll die if you don't. You know that."

"I'm not a good person," I whispered.

"Then be one," he murmured. "You can change that."

I swallowed and wiped at my eyes. "What if I don't want to? What if I like who I am?"

"In this life?" Anson stepped away from me. "Then no one can help you."

I nodded. "I don't need help. I love being here. I-I just need to prove myself."

Anson offered me a sad smile. "That kind of love will get you killed. Good luck, Isabel. You'll need it."

"I won't. Church is waiting for me. He'll help me. He loves me," I whispered. "I just need to get him to prove it to Everett." I paused. "Will you be here when I get back?"

"No," he said. "I'm done here. We won't be seeing one another again."

"Then good luck to you too, Archangel."

A tiny smile touched the corner of his lips at the nickname he was known as in the underground for his violence.

I turned away from him, now more than ever determined to bring

Church back with me. I was going to return to Chapel Crest and right a few wrongs and claim what was mine.

I'd show Everett exactly how useful I was.

SIN

She was gone.

I had no clue if she was coming back or if that was it. I didn't know if our baby was OK. I didn't know how I felt anymore. I knew fuck all.

It was driving me insane. A lot had changed over the last few days. I'd spent them holed up in my room, feeling like complete shit and questioning everything.

"Relax. She'll be back," Stitches said as I stared out at the lake. "If that's what you're thinking about."

"How do you know? She's fucking gone," I muttered. I was stoned out of my mind. Self-medicating was always a useful way to help me avoid feeling pain. In this instance, it was also keeping me from completely lashing out.

"Because she's crazy. Anyone who is crazy always ends up back here," he answered with a shrug.

Ashes winced but nodded. "He's not wrong."

I scoffed and took another hit from my weed.

"I'm trying to wrap my mind around why you want her back when she tried to cut your arm off in your sleep. Why when she was fucking Church and cheating on you. Hell, you don't even know if that baby is yours. Clearly, you can't trust her," Stitches continued, frowning at me.

"Man has a point," Ashes said.

I blew out smoke and sighed. "I don't fucking know anything anymore. I thought I did. Maybe I just need closure."

"Then get it," Church said, coming onto the patio.

I bristled at the sight of him. Images of him buried inside Bells flashed through my mind and my anger soared again.

I got to my feet and glared at him. "Don't fucking talk to me about shit."

"I'm not doing this," Ashes said, getting to his feet too. "What Church did was fucked up. Seriously, what the hell were you think-ing?" Ashes looked to Church who remained quiet. "It doesn't matter though. We're being torn apart by some girl who was hellbent on doing a lot of damage. You're both really putting me and Stitches in a shitty place neither of us wants to be in."

Stitches stood and sighed. "He's right. I'm straight up not having a good time. We're being torn apart. I know you guys can feel it happening. I'll fucking bail on you shits if you keep it up. Fucking kiss and make up or we just call it good and go our separate ways. I'm not living like this. Life is fucking bad enough. Don't add to it."

I glanced at Church, my heart in my throat. One of my biggest fears was our group disbanding. Without Bells and my brothers, I was fucking nothing. I was less than nothing. I was completely lost. The thought at losing them too made my chest constrict.

I swallowed hard.

"I-I'm mad," I said lamely.

"How about if I soothe the wounds?" Church asked, his voice soft.

"I'm listening."

"Everyone sit. It's story time," Church said, gesturing to the patio chairs.

I glanced at Ashes and Stitches who both hesitated.

"I'm serious, man. If you guys fight, I'm out. I'm not dealing with this shit," Stitches warned. "Brother or not, fuck off. Know what I mean? This shit can't keep going on."

"I'm with Stitches. I can't do it. I love you guys. Seeing this shit happen isn't cool," Ashes murmured.

"I got it. Now sit down," Church said, nodding to the chair.

We all took a seat. I couldn't force myself to look at Church, so I said nothing as I stared out at the lake.

"My father stopped in for a visit," Church started.

I shifted in my seat. Everett Church was a grade-A prick. Whenever he showed up, it meant shit was going to go down or was in the process of going down. An appearance by him was never fun.

"Bells was working for him," Church continued.

I sat up and finally looked over at him. "What?"

"He's her guardian. She's my adopted sister. She's yours too." Church looked to Stitches who stared blankly at him.

"Excuse me. What?" Stitches finally managed as I rolled Church's words around in my mind. I hadn't known her guardian. She'd refused to speak about him. Guess now I knew why.

Church launched into telling us everything his father said to him as I sat there numbly listening to it, each of his words striking me harder in the chest.

I'd been so blind to it all.

When he finished, we all sat in silence for several long moments before Ashes spoke.

"So she was tasked with getting you back home? To join up with your old man? To, like, get you to love her enough to follow?"

Church nodded, a look of disgust on his face.

I didn't know what to say to that. Did it mean she hadn't cared about me after all? So many thoughts tumbled through my head that I had a hard time on settling on one.

"I got her pregnant. She let me," I finally said. "Doesn't that mean something?"

Stitches gave me a sad look. "Not really, man. It means she fucked you more than you fucked her."

Nausea roiled low in my guts.

"If it's even yours," Church finished.

I licked my lips. "I-I don't know. It has to be. But she said she slept with someone else on campus. To-to hurt me." I hated admitting it out loud to my friends.

Ashes winced. "Damnit, man. When? Who was it with?"

"I told her I didn't want to know. I-I know that baby is mine. It has to be. She wouldn't fuck someone she wasn't with without a condom. I know her—"

"Excuse me, but you don't know shit about her," Church said. "She's fucked up."

"Well, you cheated with her, so really, what's that say about you?" I snapped at him. I had no fucking idea what I was supposed to be thinking right then. My emotions were all over the place. And so were my doubts. The baby. . . it had to be mine. It just had to be. I'd been pushing the possibility of it not being mine out of my head for weeks. If only she were here to actually tell me the truth for once.

But would it be the truth?

I didn't know shit anymore. Nothing made sense. My heart hurt. That's all I knew.

"I'm sorry I hurt you," Church murmured. He locked his green eyes on mine. "You need to know that I never wanted to hurt you. She said you had a fantasy about it. I was stupid for half a second and believed her. She told me you didn't want to talk about it, but I should have spoken to you and confirmed it. I should have told you everything, but I knew you wouldn't listen to me. I only did what I did to get you away from her. I didn't have feelings for her at all. I knew if I fucked her, you'd break it off and be free. I'm sorry, Sinclair. Truly. I did it to save you."

My throat burned as I stared at him.

He dug around in his pocket before pulling out a rabbit's paw on a keyring.

"I made this for you. I stole its luck in the hopes you'd forgive me. I want you to have it now so maybe the next time you fall in love, it'll be with a girl who loves you right back." He pushed the rabbit foot across the table.

No one said a word. I stared at it for a moment, my vision blurry with tears, before I reached out and picked it up, blinking away the moisture gathering in my eyes.

"I'm sorry too," I finally said. "For putting you guys through any of this. For. . . any and all of it. Church." I paused and gathered myself. "I-I love you. All of you."

He inclined his head at me in a quick nod. "I love you too, brother."

"Thank fuck," Stitches said, sitting back in his seat and raking his fingers through his dark hair. "You guys were stressing me out! Like, what the hell, man?"

"Me too," Ashes said, smiling. "Stitches and I were talking about getting our own dorm together. And you know how much I hate dorm rooms."

I let out a soft laugh, the act making me feel good. It had been far too long since I'd had any semblance of humor in my life.

"Now, let's talk about what we're going to do about her," Church said after another moment of silence.

"Just let her go. She'll fuck herself," Ashes said. "We get a DNA test on the baby. Then we go from there."

Church shook his head. "It's more than that. She's not just some innocent girl. She works for my father. You know what he does. Flesh trade. Cannibal market. Trafficking. The whole nine yards."

I frowned. "What aren't you saying?"

Church sighed and locked his eyes on me. "My father told me how he left her with a little girl only nights ago. He gave her permission to do whatever she wanted. He wanted to test her. To let her get her anger out. She took that permission and stomped on that little girl's head until she stopped screaming."

Ashes looked ill as Stitches blinked rapidly at the information.

I crinkled my brows and wrapped my arms around my midsection in a sad attempt to hold the nausea inside.

"How do you know he wasn't lying?" I finally managed to ask.

Church pulled out a bloody blonde ringlet and dropped it onto the table. "My father had this delivered to me today. There were photos of her with the little girl too. Holding her body." Church rubbed his eyes.

"Isabella was covered in blood. Smiling. The note from my father said, *I know you like trophies. Here's one to behold.* I have the photos if you want to see them, but they're really brutal and I don't think it's a good idea."

I got to my feet and went to the railing and vomited over the side, my head spinning.

Ashes patted my back as I heaved once more over the railing.

She was a liar. A murderer. She hurt children with the king of all monsters. Everything had been a lie.

Everything.

I straightened and wiped at my mouth. Ashes pushed a bottle of water into my hands, and I quickly swished a mouthful before spitting it out and then taking another drink, swallowing.

Calmly, I went back to my seat and sat.

"I. . . I need to think," I finally said, getting up again. All this energy was pinging through my body. Rage. Anger. Hurt. Pain. Betrayal. It was a whirlwind, and I didn't know which way to go.

"Take it easy, man," Ashes called out. "Just rest."

"Sin—" Church called out to me.

I stopped and turned to him. "We're good."

He gave me a nod. "We're good."

And we were. I forgave him. I got why he did what he did. He was trying to save me.

The problem was, I wasn't good anymore.

I was very, very bad because the thoughts rushing through my mind could get someone killed. I was a breath away from complete destruction.

BELLS

$\mathcal{I}$ stared up at the main building at Chapel Crest, loathing this place. Hating the people inside it. I'd had a bad week. Everett banished me. Sent me back here without so much as a backward glance.

I had to prove to him I wasn't worthless. I hated feeling like I was. I'd done everything he'd wanted. At least I thought I had. My plan was simple. I was going to get rid of Sin and claim Church.

I'd already taken care of the baby Sin had put inside me. The last thing I wanted was a reminder of him in my life. I was positive the baby was his. Of course, there was that small chance it was Asylum's. Either way, it was another problem gone.

A smile touched my lips at the thought of Church buried deep inside me. Soon, he'd be mine for good.

I went straight to the watchers' house. Anger and hatred rose inside me the closer I got to their place. Thoughts on losing Everett raced through my mind. Thoughts on Sin ruining my life. Making me have his piece of shit baby. Like the world needed another one of him in it. He ruined everything, especially with Church.

I'd had him. I'd had Church. Letting that go wasn't an option. I'd kill Sin if I had to.

I stopped along the path to the house and went to a rock on the edge of the trail. Lifting it, I pulled out a knife I kept there. If shit went south, I'd stab Sin until he stopped breathing. I'd finish the job his father had been too weak to do.

I slid the knife up my sleeve to conceal it. When I got to their house, I knocked on the door. A moment later, Sin answered.

He looked like hell. His usual sexiness was gone. He kept the sides of his head shaven with the center long, which he piled atop his head in a man bun. His blond hair lay limp around his shoulders, the glimmer in his gray eyes gone. He even appeared thinner.

He was broken.

Good. Fuck him. I wasn't done yet. I was sure there were more pieces to shatter.

"What do you want?" he asked, his voice wobbling.

"Church."

He snorted at me. "Get lost, Bells. He's not interested."

"His dick said another story," I countered. "You know. When he was fucking me and trying to make me come on it."

Sin visibly shook, making me smirk. He stepped outside the screen door.

"Get the fuck out of here."

"You know what? Fuck you. I'm not leaving until I see him."

"Bells, now isn't a good time. Just. . . go back to your dorm. I'm really upset with you—"

"What's wrong, Sin? Did I hurt your poor, little feelings when I fucked your friend?"

"Bells, please." He winced, the pain clear on his face. "Just go. I can't look at you right now."

"Good thing I'm not here for you, you worthless sack of shit." I made to push past him to go into the house, but he was quick to stop me and block the door.

"No, Bells. You need to leave."

I ground my teeth and tugged a piece of paper out of my pocket. "Here, you piece of shit."

"What's this?" He unfolded it and frowned down as his gray eyes roved over the bill for services.

"Your dad should have finished the job," I said, venom dripping from every word. "It's my abortion bill. Since you didn't die, I killed your fucking kid."

The paper fluttered out of his hands and landed on the steps. A tear trickled from his eye as his hands shook.

"I hate you, Sinclair. I've never hated someone as much as I hate you. Even the men who touched me. I still hold them in higher regard than I'll ever hold you. You're less than nothing. No one will ever want you. You're not worthy of shit in this life or the next. You should have died all those years ago when your father shot you. He died in vain."

Ashes came out of the house and moved quickly past Sin and shoved me hard in the chest. I stumbled backward off the step as he kept advancing on me. Stitches came out and wrapped his arm around Sin's shoulders and talked to him in a low voice.

But Ashes. . . he was pissed.

I'd never seen him that way before. He was the nicer one out of all of them.

He shoved me again, and I pulled out my knife and snarled at him.

"Get fucking lost, you cunt," he spat at me, not phased by my move.

I swung my knife at him. He dodged me easily before he grabbed my arm and bent it painfully behind my back. I let out a cry as he tightened his hold and chicken-winged my arm. Searing agony raced through me as he jacked up my arm further, his lips at my ear, the knife having fallen to the ground.

"You just signed your own death warrant. No one fucks with a watcher."

"Fuck you," I rasped. "Church won't let that happen."

"Church doesn't control my fucking lighter. Before this is over, I'll have your ashes on my hands and not one fucking regret about it. If you come back here, I will kill you." His words were soft and fierce, filled with a promise that made me shudder. "Don't fuck with Sin ever again."

"I'll kill him," I whimpered. "If you let me go, I'll fucking kill him."

Ashes chuckled softly in my ear, sending more goosebumps erupting over my skin.

"And I'll take your knife and carve new holes in your body and fuck every one of them before I set you on fire. Don't fucking try me, Isabella." He shoved me forward and I hit the ground hard, letting out a hiss of pain on impact.

I climbed to my feet, my body trembling, to see Sin and Stitches were no longer on the step. They'd gone inside. It was just me and Ashes.

He leveled his gaze on me. He was taunting me. Promising me pain.

I took a step away from him. He was terrifying in that moment.

I glanced to my knife at his feet. He bent low and picked it up before giving it an elaborate twirl between his fingers, no emotion on his pretty face.

So Ashes liked knives and fire.

Good to know.

I'd be sure he wasn't around when I made my next move.

"I'll be back," I said fiercely.

"I'll be waiting," he answered.

We glared at one another for a moment before I turned and left, my fury intensified.

I hadn't signed my death warrant. Both Ashes and Sin had signed theirs. Sin wouldn't be hard to kill. Ashes might be.

It didn't matter. I'd end them both for fucking with me.

That was a promise I intended on keeping.

CHURCH

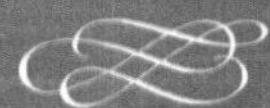

I was sick to my stomach as I watched Sin stare out at the lake, tears in his eyes. It had been two days since Bells visited. We'd heard him crying in his room since it happened. He wasn't eating either. I knew he'd wanted that damn baby. He was desperate to love and be loved. He just didn't realize he was already loved by us. I knew it wasn't enough for him. I understood that. Hell, I lived that. I had no one but the watchers too. Having Bells's and my actions nearly tear us apart had hurt like hell.

There was no other choice though. Sin wasn't going to see reason. I had to do what I did to save him from her.

My father… that fucking prick. He needed to go too.

I promised myself at some point he would. When I was stronger and had more going for me. Right now, I was still young and had a lot more planning to do.

Of course, that also gave him time to plan.

Sin didn't bother wiping the tears that trailed down his cheeks away.

I looked to Stitches to see the pained expression on his face. Bells had hurt all of us through using Sin.

"She has to go," Ashes said softly, ending the silence as we sat on our patio overlooking the lake that evening. "She said she's going to kill Sin. I'm pretty sure I'm on her list now too."

Stitches raked his fingers through his hair and sat back in his seat, his arms crossed over his chest.

I didn't get a chance to speak because Sin did.

"Let's kill her," he said softly, not tearing his focus from the lake.

"I'm in," I murmured. "She hurt you. She's planning on hurting Ashes. She's hurt children. She works with my father. I don't see one redeeming quality about her."

"I'm in too," Stitches said.

"How are we going to do it?" Ashes looked at me. "What's the plan?"

"It's simple," I said as Sin finally turned and joined us. He wiped at his eyes, a look of determination on his face. He'd been so withdrawn. So broken. I fucking hated that for him. He wasn't that guy. At least he hadn't been before that bitch came into his life.

"She wants me. I'll lure her in," I continued. I looked to see Sin's reaction.

His face remained emotionless. "Bring her to the house. I want to be the one to do it. For my kid."

I nodded. "OK."

"I'll burn her body. Most of her will become ash. We can take care of what's left," Ashes added, flicking his lighter open and closed. Five times. Open. Close. Open Close. He let the flame go, illuminating his face. He was dead fucking serious on this.

So was I.

"I'll punch her in the cunt," Stitches said. "If there's time for that."

I shot him a quick grin, and he winked at me.

"So it's settled." Sin cleared his throat, his hands visibly shaking. "When will we do it?"

I looked to Ashes. "Do you need anything for the fire?"

"Just a fucking body," he said, offering me a sinister smile.

I grinned widely at him before taking in my watchers' faces. "Tomorrow. We kill her tomorrow."

I placed my hand on the center of the round patio table. Sin rested his hand over mine, his eyes locked on me. I gave him a nod as Ashes put his hand over Sin's, followed by Stitches finishing it off.

"Always together," I whispered, stating our vow we had.

"Never apart." Sin visibly swallowed.

"Through whatever weather," Ashes murmured.

"From the endings to the start," Stitches finished.

"One more thing," I said before our hands were separated. "We vow from here on out that we claim one girl together. No more separate women. We find one and we keep her. For all of us. I don't want this shit to ever happen again. Agreed?"

"Agreed," Stitches said immediately.

"Agreed." Ashes looked to Sin. "Sin?"

He cleared his throat. "Share a girl? Between all of us?"

I nodded.

Sin licked his lips. "I'll never love anyone ever again. I have no desire to."

"You will, brother," Ashes murmured. "I promise you that. She's out there, and she'll be perfect for all of us. She'll complete us."

Sin's hand trembled over mine. "I-I. . ."

"Together, Sinclair," I said.

He locked eyes with me. "Together." He nodded. "I-I agree."

"So be it," I whispered, a thrill rushing through me. I hadn't killed a person in months. The fact it was going to be this bitch excited me.

How many lives were we saving by ending hers?

The answer was simple. Four. Ours. Because we were saving each other.

BELLS

Someone dropped a note on my desk as I sat in Sister Elizabeth's class. I glanced at the person to see it was some guy named Bryce. I rolled my eyes, assuming he was being cryptic about asking me out or something.

Three days ago I'd told Sin everything I'd wanted to say to him. I'd watched him waver and crumble. I was overly satisfied and felt nothing over the incident except my rage. I wanted him dead. I wanted Asher Valentine dead. Both would be excellent trophies to take home to Everett.

With Church at my side, I knew Everett would welcome me back if I brought him the bodies of the watchers. And since Stitches was already his son through adoption, we could be one happy family like Everett had intended in the beginning.

It was perfect.

I unfolded the paper to see a handwritten note.

Meet me tonight at my place. We'll be alone. We can finish what we started.

-Church

My heart jumped in my chest. I'd won. I'd finally won. Church wanted me. He'd come to his senses. I'd get to go home with my prize.

Quickly, I gathered my things and left the room as Sister Elizabeth called out to me to get back there. There was no fucking way I was going back. I was going to get my love. My Church.

"It'll be hard to breathe," Asylum's voice came out.

I glanced to see him coming out from an alley between two buildings. He fell in step with me.

"Not now," I muttered. "I don't have time for your crazy."

"Now is the only time we have."

I ignored him.

"Do you want to die, Ding Dong?"

I stopped and spun to face him. "Why are you harassing me?"

"Is that what I'm doing?" He blinked his icy blue eyes at me and cocked his head. "You killed the baby."

"That's not the only thing I'm going to kill."

"You're a wicked soul, Isabella. Sophia. The little girl. Did she scream?"

"Until the end," I muttered, rolling my eyes at him. "Why? Does that get you off?"

"No. I'm not you," he said softly. "I get off on many things. Except that."

I rolled my eyes at him. "Say what you need to say. I've got more important things to do than deal with you."

"I was just going to warn you. . . but I think I'll let you go. Some of us deserve to win sometimes." His brows crinkled and he cocked his head again. "She's coming. Who? Who is she?"

"What?" I frowned at him. "Tell your voices to shut the fuck up."

He tugged at his hair for a moment. "Everything is so. . . foggy."

"Go take your meds."

His blue eyes snapped to mine and he smiled, his demeanor changing. "I never take meds. I'm sane as can be." He pointed to his head and grinned wider. "This is just for funsies."

"Whatever," I muttered. "I gotta go."

"It'll hurt, Ding Dong. Then it'll *burn*."

"Then I guess I'll see you in hell, *Asylum*."

He smirked at me, his blue eyes twinkling, and inclined his head.

"See you in hell, Ding Dong." He turned and walked away, whistling that strange song I'd heard him hum before. I shook my head and sighed. He was what crazy looked like. Not me.

I went to my dorm and showered and did my makeup and picked out an outfit to wear for Church. He liked a lot of black, so I put on a long, black dress and fluffed my blonde hair. Waiting around until nightfall was awful, but I managed it. The moment the sun disappeared off the horizon, I left my room and took the wooded trail past the cemetery to the watchers' house.

I fluffed my hair again and knocked on the door.

It opened a moment later, Church greeting me in all black.

He stepped aside for me to come in.

Once inside, he closed the door softly behind me as I took in our surroundings. He had candles going throughout the darkened room, illuminating it in a soft glow.

"It's beautiful," I said, smiling up at him as I rested my hands on his chest.

"I thought you may enjoy your last night in this house with candles," he said, his voice low.

"Why? Because you're coming home with me? Back to Everett?"

He nodded. "I am. I've realized I've been overlooking the most important things in my life. My home. My family."

I crushed my lips against his. He didn't touch me, but he did kiss me back, sending a thrill through me.

Church said he never kissed, but he was kissing me. I'd definitely won.

God, he was a good kisser. Full, soft lips. Teeth. A growl.

I was in heaven.

"Come," he said against my lips. "Let's go to my room. I don't want anyone to hear you screaming."

I nodded eagerly, letting him lead me upstairs.

The moment we were in his room, my mouth was back on his, my hands all over him. He still didn't touch me, but I knew he would. Maybe he was nervous to be with me.

I deepened the kiss, tasting his tongue against mine. He was minty and sweet.

"I love you," I choked out between kisses. "I've loved you for so long, Dante."

He grunted again before I smashed my lips back on his.

"Tell me you love me too," I begged softly, breaking off the kiss. "Please tell me."

He smiled down at me. "Oh, Isabella."

My heartbeat thundered as I waited for his words.

He lifted a blonde wave off my shoulder and rubbed it between his thumb and index finger, a tiny smile on his face.

"I fucking hate you," he finished.

I didn't get to react. I was yanked back, a cord around my neck. I stared wide-eyed at him as I struggled against my attacker, my fingers aching as much as my neck as I tried to break the tension cutting off my air supply.

Church moved closer to me as the cord tightened, sending black sparks flying over my vision.

He stared down at me, smiling as my vision continued to darken.

"No one fucks with a watcher," he said. "And lives to tell about it."

I stopped my bucking and struggling and reached out for him as he took a step away.

"Finish her, Sin."

Sin. Sin. SIN!

It was a set-up. They were. . . killing me.

No. God! Please, no! I'm sorry! I'm so sorry! Let me speak. Please, let me tell them I won't do it again. That I want to live. That I'm. . .

My body weakened as I sagged against Sin. He maintained his hold on me.

"Sweet dreams, Bells," he whispered in my ear as a dull roar filled my ears.

I locked my eyes on Church who simply stared back at me, no emotion on his face.

My eyelids shuttered. My body twitched. Church became blurry before he faded out completely.

Then. . .
Darkness.

SIN

$\mathcal{I}$ stared at Bells's lifeless body on the ground at my feet, the watchers at my side. She'd struggled to live. It was almost too much for me to complete, but I'd done it, knowing she would have really tried to kill me and Ashes if given the chance. That I was saving lives by ending hers, especially since Everett had his claws deep in her.

No more innocent people needed to be harmed.

I'd done the world a favor.

At least that's what I kept telling myself.

But fuck, it hurt. I tried to shut everything down so I wasn't feeling, but it wasn't working. I hated myself for ever loving her. For ever thinking she could love me. For losing my baby. For everything.

I hated *me*.

She'd been right. I was a monster. I was worthless. I was a killer. A murderer. A piece of shit. I'd become her in order to stop her. Did that make me better? Not in my mind.

"You don't have to stay for this part," Ashes said from my right.

"No." I swallowed hard. "I'll stay."

Church and Stitches hadn't said a word. Even when Bells had died in Church's room, he simply reached out and squeezed my shoulder.

Stitches and Ashes had come into the room and helped move her body out to the car so we could take her to Ashes's special hot spot. I was a fucking wreck. I had been useless moving her. Not that she was heavy, but my heart couldn't take it.

I'd killed her. I'd murdered her.

She was dead because of me.

That's just what my love got me. Murder. Nearly losing my family.

Ashes stepped forward with Stitches and they lifted Bells up and dropped her body in the metal burning barrel Ashes had acquired from god knew where. It was new and larger than his others. She fit nearly perfectly inside it, her blonde hair still spilling over the edge, her feet barely visible as her body bent to fit.

It was an ugly funeral. An ugly burial.

I had no idea what Ashes had put in the barrel to burn with her, but I watched as he tossed a lit match inside and it erupted in brilliant orange and red flames that licked the night sky.

The heat from the fire was so hot, we had to step back several feet. None of us spoke for hours as we stood and watched her burn.

Silent sentries, guarding the dead.

We were depraved. Sick. But we were patients at Chapel Crest. We weren't students here. Students learned. Patients suffered.

And we suffered as we watched Bells burn in that barrel.

For hours.

In silence.

Her hair ignited. Her skin melted.

And she slowly turned to ash just like Ashes had promised.

The flames gave way to smoke before it became nothing.

It had been all night, but felt like only minutes.

Ashes stepped forward and went to the barrel and peered inside it. I looked away, my stomach sick.

Stitches and him spoke, and I heard the sound of a plastic bag.

"You'll be OK," Church murmured to me.

I nodded, my throat tight.

"She deserved this kind of love," he continued. "You know she did. It's over now. You're free. So is she."

I nodded again, unable to speak.

Church squeezed my shoulder before he tugged me to him and wrapped his arms around me in a tight embrace. I sobbed softly in his arms, holding him back.

"It's over, Sinclair. A new story begins today. It'll be the best story ever told. I promise you that, brother. Do you believe me?"

"Yes," I rasped in a wobbly voice as I clung to him. "I believe you."

"Together."

"Never apart,"I whispered.

"Through whatever weather," Ashes said, joining us and wrapping his arms around us.

"From the endings to the start." Stitches's head rested against mine, his warm hand on my back.

"I love you guys," I choked out. "Thank you."

"We love you too," Church answered.

We stayed holding each other for a long time until we broke apart. Ashes bent and picked up a small box and handed it to me.

I took it, breathing hard.

"Some bone is left," Ashes said gently. "The fire took care of the rest. We can scatter the ashes on the lake, but you'll need to dispose of what's left."

"Take her remains and put them somewhere only you know," Church said. "Don't tell anyone, not even us, where they are."

I nodded. I knew just the place.

"Yeah," I managed to say.

It was a fitting end it seemed with the ashes since that lake had been my solace through all of this. As for the bone, well, every skeleton had a closet. Or floorboard.

✝

I SLID the floorboard back in place in Sully's office after the day had spun into night to ensure I wouldn't be seen. We'd dumped Bells's ashes on the lake earlier that morning after we'd gotten home. No one said anything to mourn her. We'd simply gone back to the house and sat in silence.

I'd only whispered goodbye as the lake lapped up what was left of her.

I didn't know what drove me to putting Bells's remains in Sully's office, but something told me it was the perfect spot, so that's where I was. Should the event ever arise if questions were asked, Sully would have to take the fall.

Nothing would happen though.

Everett would see to it.

I was certain he'd planned this entire thing out. Bells. Her murder. Church helping. I'd thought about it the entire way to Sully's. He wanted Church to snap and do the deeds he did. It brought him closer to insanity. Church always teetered on the line.

Everett knew that.

I was nearly certain that's all this was. Everett never cared for Bells. She was just a tool for him to use to get to Church. Everett Church played the long game. He always had.

It always worked too.

I think Church knew it was part of Everett's plan. The thing Everett didn't plan on was that Church played long games too. He was to be feared. Everett just didn't know how much yet.

I got to my feet and left the room and went home. I bypassed going inside and simply walked to the back patio and sat in my chair and stared out at the lake.

Nothing made sense.

Everything I'd felt before was gone, leaving me to feel hollow and empty. I only knew one thing though.

I'd never love anyone ever again.

Maybe I was a student at Chapel Crest because I'd learned a lesson.

But I was also very much a patient here too.

I was crazy enough to do anything now to keep my family safe.

To keep us together. A girl for all of us would only wreck us. I felt that to my very bones. I'd never let another girl come between us again.

"Never apart," I whispered the words like a prayer. "I'll protect us."

A-fucking-men.

163

The End. . . And Beginning.

Thank you for reading Bells: The Boys of Chapel Crest. Please consider leaving your review.
Be sure to get Ashes: The Boys of Chapel Crest here: Ashes: The Boys of Chapel Crest

ACKNOWLEDGMENTS

Thank you to my alpha readers. You guys rock.

Thanks to Mr. K.G. for all he does.

Thanks to JA Roles for always listening to me freak out about deadlines.

Thanks to Charlotte for helping me when I'm ready to tear my hair out.

Thanks to the Discord members for always making me laugh with all the wild theories. I love them all.

Thanks to my street team, TikTok team, ARC readers, and everyone who has had a hand in some way to help me out. I appreciate you all.

As always, thank you to my readers. You guys make every word worth it.

Riot's dad goes to Mayfair and plays an instrument. His mom attended Bolten and plays for both warring sides. No one ever reads these, right?

ABOUT THE AUTHOR

Affectionately dubbed Queen of Cliffies, Suspense, Heartbreak, and Torture by her readers, USA Today and International Bestselling author K.G. Reuss is known mostly for making readers ugly cry with her writing. A cemetery creeper and ghost enthusiast, K.G. spends most of her time toeing the line between imagination and forced adulthood.

After a stint in college in Iowa, K.G. moved back to her home in Michigan to work in emergency medicine. She's currently raising three small ghouls and is married to a vampire overlord.

K.G. is the author of the Black Falls High series, Kings of Bolten, the Boys of Chapel Crest, The Everlasting Chronicles, Emissary of the Devil, The Chronicles of Winterset, and many more with a ridiculous amount of other series set to be released.

Sign up for her newsletter to stay updated on all the things happening in her freakishly ghoulish world. https://tinyletter.com/authorkgreuss

Can't get enough? Visit her website at www.kgreuss.com or join her reader group on Facebook: K.G. Reuss's Renegade Readers

ALSO BY K.G REUSS

May We Rise

As We Fight

On The Edge

When We Fall

Double Dare You

Double Dare Me

Church: The Boys of Chapel Crest

Ashes: The Boys of Chapel Crest

Stitches: The Boys of Chapel Crest

Emissary of the Devil: Testimony of the Damned

Emissary of the Devil: Testimony of the Blessed

The Everlasting Chronicles: Dead Silence

The Everlasting Chronicles: Shadow Song

The Everlasting Chronicles: Grave Secrets

The Everlasting Chronicles: Soul Bound

The Chronicles of Winterset: Oracle

The Chronicles of Winterset: Tempest

Black Falls High: In Ruins

Black Falls High: In Silence

Black Falls High: In Chaos

Black Falls High: In Pieces, A Novella

Hard Pass

Kings of Bolten: Dirty Little Secrets

Kings of Bolten: Pretty Little Sins

Kings of Bolten: Deadly Little Promises

Kings of Bolten: Perfect Little Revenge

Kings of Bolten: Savage Little Queen

<u>Barely Breathing</u>

<u>The Middle Road</u>

<u>Seven Minutes in Heaven</u>